Chickie checkout

I turned back to the interior of the car and, uh, hopped my front feet up on the seat.

Hmmmmm!

There, my eyes fell upon a box, a cute little cardboard box ... with holes in the sides. And coming from inside the cute little box were ... uh ... cute little chirping sounds. Gee whiz, I wondered, what could be causing those, uh, sounds. I mean, I had encountered many cardboard boxes in the course of my career, but never one that ... well, cheeped and chirped.

I cast one more glance toward the, uh, people ... Sally May and Alfred, shall we say ... and they were still deeply involved in their conversation about cages and so forth, and obviously had no time to be bothered with—

I inched my way deeper into the car, this time daring to bring my hind legs off the ground and onto the floorboard. I pointed my nose toward the box. Slurp, slurp. The waterworks of my mouth were suddenly ... I had to activate Tongulary Pumps to clear out all the water from ...

I steered my nose to the box and positioned it right under the lid. We had contact! I punched in the commands for Silent Hydraulic Nose Lift, and slowly, very slowly, the lid of the box began to—

"Hank!"

The Case of the
Tender Cheeping Chickies

John R. Erickson

Illustrations by Gerald L. Holmes

PUFFIN BOOKS

PUFFIN BOOKS
Published by the Penguin Group
Penguin Young Readers Group, 345 Hudson Street, New York, New York 10014, U.S.A.
Penguin Group (Canada), 90 Eglinton Avenue East, Suite 700, Toronto, Ontario,
Canada M4P 2Y3 (a division of Pearson Penguin Canada Inc.)
Penguin Books Ltd, 80 Strand, London WC2R 0RL, England
Penguin Ireland, 25 St Stephen's Green, Dublin 2, Ireland
(a division of Penguin Books Ltd)
Penguin Group (Australia), 250 Camberwell Road, Camberwell, Victoria 3124, Australia
(a division of Pearson Australia Group Pty Ltd)
Penguin Books India Pvt Ltd, 11 Community Centre, Panchsheel Park,
New Delhi - 110 017, India
Penguin Group (NZ), Cnr Airborne and Rosedale Roads, Albany,
Auckland 1310, New Zealand (a division of Pearson New Zealand Ltd)
Penguin Books (South Africa) (Pty) Ltd, 24 Sturdee Avenue, Rosebank,
Johannesburg 2196, South Africa

Registered Offices: Penguin Books Ltd, 80 Strand, London WC2R 0RL, England

Published simultaneously in the United States of America by Viking
and Puffin Books, divisions of Penguin Young Readers Group, 2006

1 3 5 7 9 10 8 6 4 2

LIBRARY OF CONGRESS CATALOGING-IN-PUBLICATION DATA

Erickson, John R., date.
The case of the tender cheeping chickies / by John R. Erickson ;
illustrations by Gerald L. Holmes.
p. cm.—(Hank the Cowdog ; 47)
Summary: In the course of his job as Head of Ranch Security, Hank the dog is asked to
guard five chicks, despite the fact that poultry is his favorite kind of dinner.
ISBN 0-14-240553-1 (pbk.)—ISBN 0-670-06097-6 (hardcover)
[1. Chickens—Fiction. 2. Dogs—Fiction. 3. Ranch life—West (U.S.)—Fiction.
4. West (U.S.)—Fiction. 5. Humorous stories. 6. Mystery and detective stories.]
I. Holmes, Gerald L., ill. II. Title.
PZ7.E72556Casm 2006 [Fic]—dc22 2005051531

Hank the Cowdog® is a registered trademark of John R. Erickson.

Printed in the United States of America

To the good people of my hometown,
Perryton, Texas, who were the first
to recognize something special in Hank.

CONTENTS

CHAPTER ONE

The Eternal
Bedsprings Mystery

It's me again, Hank the Cowdog. The Long-Snouted Road Monster attacked our ranch early one morning in the spring. We had no warning whatsoever. One minute, everything was quiet and peaceful. The next minute, the peace and quiet were ripped apart by the roar of the monster.

Maybe you don't believe in Long-Snouted Road Monsters. Well, I didn't believe in 'em either, until this one attacked our headquarters compound and threatened to tear the place to smithereens and eat every person and dog on the ranch.

As you can see, this will be no ordinary mystery. On a scale of one to ten, it scores a 9.5 in

1

Chills and Nightmares. It's so bad, we'll have to check IDs. No kidding. It's that scary.

Or, tell you what, if you're underage, sickly, or nervous, skip the first three chapters and pick up the story in Chapter Four. That'll get you through the roughest parts.

Okay, where were we? Oh yes, the baby chicks. They came to the ranch in a cardboard box with holes in the sides. Little Alfred and his mom bought them at a farm where hens sit on nests, lay eggs, and hatch out baby chickens.

Baby chickens come from eggs. Did you know that? Maybe you thought that bacon comes from eggs, but that's incorrect. Bacon comes from pigs, and baby chicks come from eggs, but bacon and eggs are sometimes found together in breakfast situations because . . .

Wait a minute, hold everything. We weren't talking about the baby chicks. They come in later in the story, and to be honest, you're not supposed to know anything about them yet.

So forget we said anything about baby chicks or bacon and eggs, even though baby chicks really do come from eggs, and bacon really does . . . uh . . . make my mouth water.

Just skip it. We never said anything about the so forth.

We were talking about the Long-Snouted Road Monster, is what we were talking about, so sit down and prepare yourself for some Heavy-Duty Scary Stuff.

It all began on a quiet morning in the springtime. I've already said that, but I don't care. It never hurts to repeat important important facts facts, because by their very nature, they are very important.

It was a quiet morning on the ranch, just another average springtime day. The wild turkeys had come off their roost at daylight and had gobbled their usual nonsense to who—or whomever—listens to such rubbish, not me, because a turkey has nothing to say that I want to hear.

Oh, and I had done my usual job of barking the sun over the horizon, which is a very important part of my daily routine. If I ever skipped a day, there wouldn't be a day. Every day would be a night, because any day without sunlight is no day at all. Also, if I ever skipped a day of Barking Up the Sun, the turkeys would have nothing to gobble about, because they always gobble first thing in the morning.

Why? I have no idea. Do I care? No. If you ask me, the world would be a better place if those guys didn't make all that noise in the early-morning hours. It's not that they disturb my sleep, because I'm very seldom asleep at that hour. Okay, sometimes I am asleep at that hour and I don't appreciate . . .

Forget the turkeys.

The Road Monster Report came in around nine on a Wednesday morning. Or was it ten on a Thursday morning? It doesn't matter. The report came in, loud and clear.

Drover and I were busy, very busy, doing some important work near the corrals, although I can't remember exactly . . . wait! Here we go. Drover had just made an interesting discovery. Most of his "discoveries" aren't so interesting, but this one was.

He had discovered a big green bullfrog sitting on the south bank of Emerald Pond. Do you see the significance of this? Maybe not, so here's the scoop on that. Emerald Pond belongs to us dogs. It's our own private bath and spa, a place where the employees of the Security Division can go to relax, soak up the mineral waters, and recover from the grinding routine of running our ranch.

In other words, it's our private retreat and vacation spot, yet, according to Drover's report, a big fat ugly green frog was sitting on the southern shore—and looking very satisfied about it, as though he owned the place. Well, he *didn't* own the place, and to be very blunt about it, he hadn't even been invited to use our facilities.

When Drover brought me the news about the trespassing frog, I was shocked and dismayed. "A frog using our facilities? That's no good, son. I hope you ordered him to leave."

Drover gave me a silly grin. "Yep, it never hurts to hope."

"Does that mean you ordered him to leave?"

"Well ... not exactly. It means that hope makes eternal bedsprings."

There was a moment of silence. "What?"

"I said ... let me think here. There's an old saying about hope and bedsprings."

"Yes? Go on. Explain yourself."

"Well ... I'd sure hate to mess it up." Drover twisted his face into a wad of concentration. "Eternal bedsprings are made of hope."

"Eternal bedsprings? I've never heard of such a thing. Is it possible ... wait, hold everything. I just figured it out." I began pacing back and forth in front of the runt, as I often do when my mind is on the trail of an important concept. "The wise old saying to which you referred goes like this: 'Hope springs eternal.'"

"That's what I said."

"That's not what you said. You garbled it so that it came out saying something about bed-springs."

"Maybe it was a mattress."

"It wasn't a mattress, and it has nothing to do with a bed."

"Yeah, but if a bed *didn't* have any springs, wouldn't it be hard?"

"Of course. Yes. It would be very hard."

He grinned. "Well, that's why they're called 'eternal springs.' They're so hard, they last forever."

I stopped pacing and beamed him a glare. "Drover, please. You're embarrassing me. The wise old saying to which you referred has nothing to do with beds, mattresses, or eternal bed-springs. Let me repeat the wise old saying: 'Hope springs eternal.'"

A light seemed to come on in his eyes. "Oh, I get it now! The water in Emerald Pond comes from underground springs, and if you take the 'e' out of 'hope,' it's 'hop.'"

"I'm not following this, Drover."

"Water comes from springs and frogs hop, so the wise old saying was really talking about that frog I saw."

This was beginning to sound interesting. "What about 'eternal'?"

His smile faded. "I'm not sure. It doesn't fit."

"No, it doesn't. Maybe you should just drop it."

"Yeah, maybe somebody made a mistake."

"Right. It happens all the time. Okay, now we're cooking. We'll cross out the 'e' in 'hope' and drop 'eternal.' That gives us 'hop springs.'" I pondered those two words for a moment. "Wait a minute, Drover! I think I've just figured this out."

"I thought I figured it out."

"You were close, son, but in this business, close doesn't count." I resumed my pacing. "Okay, here we go, and listen carefully. Many years ago, when the Pilgrims first came to the Texas Panhandle, they discovered Emerald Pond, only back then it *didn't* have a name."

"I wonder why."

"Because it didn't, that's why. And they saw a frog sitting beside the pond, and when they walked up, the hog fropped away."

"So they called it Hog Heaven?"

I stopped in my tracks. "What? Hog Heaven? What are you talking about?"

"Well, you said they found a hog."

"I did NOT say hog. I said frog. Isn't that what we've been talking about for the past ten

minutes? Why do you bring up hogs when we're talking about frogs?"

"Well, I thought ... boy, I sure get confused."

"Hear me out, Drover, I'm very close to wrapping this thing up. Okay, when the frog hopped away, they decided to name the place Hop Springs."

"Gosh. You mean ..."

"Exactly. The old saying 'Hope springs eternal' is really a code name for Emerald Pond, dating back thousands of years. And through clever interrogation, I have pulled this secret message out of your unconscious mind. Is that awesome or what?"

"Boy, that's an old frog."

I stared at him for a moment, wondering if he knew what he'd just said. In the course of his jabbering, he had somehow managed to unearth the last piece of the puzzle.

"And now, Drover, I can reveal the rest of the mystery, for you see, I have just figured out why the word 'eternal' appeared in the wise old saying. 'Eternal' means old, right? The frog has been here for thousands of years, right?"

"Oh my gosh! You mean ..."

"Yes, Drover. We thought 'eternal' was just a mistake, but it wasn't. It was embedded into the wise old saying for a reason."

"Embedded. You mean . . . bedsprings?"

The air hissed out of my lungs. "No, Drover, and please don't mention bedsprings again."

"Sorry."

"I know you're trying to help, but just let me finish. The Pilgrims knew the frog would grow older with time and would become a very old frog, so they named our pond Eternal Hop Springs." I beamed him a triumphant smile. "So there you are. Now we know the true meaning of the wise old saying, and also how our pond got its original name."

Drover blinked his eyes several times. "I'll be derned. That's pretty amazing."

"Of course it is, but let me remind you that doing amazing things is just part of our job with the Security Division. Nice work, son. With no help at all from outside sources, we dogs have pieced together the history of Emerald Pond. What do you say we celebrate by taking a little dip in that very same pond? I'd say we've earned—" My keen eyes had just picked up an important detail: Drover wasn't smiling anymore. "What's wrong with you?"

"Oh my gosh! I just had a terrible thought!"

CHAPTER TWO

We Defeat a Smart-Aleck Frog

Are you ready to hear Drover's terrible thought? Here's what he said, word for word. "If that frog's been there for ten thousand years, wouldn't it mean that ... it's *his* pond, and not ours?"

I stared into the vacuum of his eyes. "Drover, how many times have I warned you about asking questions I can't answer?"

"I don't know. Three?"

"No. Three hundred. I've warned you over and over: Never ask questions unless they've been approved by the Head of Ranch Security. Do you see what you've done?"

"Not really."

"You've ruined everything! How can we enjoy a romp in our pond if it's not our pond?"

"Well, I guess we could ... ask the frog's permission."

"What? Ask the frog's ... Drover, I will never ask a frog's permission for anything, never!" I marched a few steps away. My mind was racing over the many details of property law. "Okay, I think I've got the answer to this."

"Oh, good."

"It's very simple. We'll approach the frog in a kind and reasonable manner, and we'll tell him to ... well ... move out, leave our pond, and never come back."

"Yeah, but what if he doesn't?"

"In that case, Drover, we'll resort to the bottom line of property law. We'll beat him up. We're bigger than he is, and we've got him outnumbered."

"Yeah, and it might be fun, 'cause frogs don't bite."

"Exactly my point. Come on, son, let's get this thing settled once and for all. The nerve of that frog, trying to steal our pond!"

We marched down to the banks of Emerald Pond, and sure enough, there he was—a big fat green bullfrog, sitting on the edge of the water.

He looked very smug and sure of himself, just the kind of frog who needed a few lessons from the School of Hard Knots.

I halted our column and gave Drover the signal to be quiet while I did the talking. I moved a few steps closer and gave the frog a friendly smile.

"Good morning, froggie. Nice day, huh? Listen, bud, I've got a little favor to ask. I wonder if you'd mind moving out of our pond and never coming back." No response. I mean, the frog didn't even look at me. He just sat there. "Smart guy, huh? Okay, pal, we tried the course of reason. Now we'll go to sterner measures. Drover, get him!"

Drover stared at me. "Me? What about the mud?"

"The mud is muddy. So what? Jump in there and beat him up!"

"Well, you know, this old leg's been giving me fits, and I'm not sure—"

"Drover, this is your big chance to rack up some Combat Points. It'll look great on your record."

"Yeah, but . . . what if he's really a handsome prince?"

I couldn't believe my ears. "A handsome prince! Drover, look at him. Is he handsome?"

"Well . . ."

"No. He's a frog, and he's even uglier than you."

"Yeah, but they can change—I've heard all those stories—and if he turned out to be a handsome prince . . . they have swords and knives and . . . oh, my leg! It's killing me!"

He began limping around in a circle and then—you won't believe this part—and then he fell over on his back and began kicking his legs in the air. I heaved a sigh and shook my head.

"Drover, I'm very disappointed in your behavior."

"I know, I'm a failure, but this old leg—"

"It's disgraceful beyond words. Okay, I'll do your dirty work, but I must warn you. This will go into my report."

"Oh no, not that!"

"Yes, Drover, every word of it. I'm sorry, but the world must know that you're not just an ordinary weenie. You're a chicken weenie who's afraid of a frog."

"Oh, the guilt! Oh, my leg!"

"Now pay attention and I'll give you a few lessons on beating up fat arrogant frogs." I turned my massive body forty-three degrees to the left and began punching in the targeting data. Behind the computer screen of my mind, I could hear Data Control chewing on the numbers. Then the secret targeting information flashed across the screen.

Do I dare reveal our targeting codes? They're pretty complicated and highly classified. I guess it wouldn't hurt to give you a little peek, but don't go blabbing this stuff around. Here's the very message that flashed across the screen of my mind:

"*JUMP.*"

There it was! Data Control had crunched all the numbers, and we had our plan of battle locked into the computer, and now it was time to launch the weapon.

I went into a Deep Crouch Position, sprang upward and outward, and launched myself right into the middle of that . . .

SPLAT!

. . . Green yucko mud where the alleged frog had been only seconds before. Do you see the meaning of this? The frog had cheated! Perhaps he had broken into our data systems and desniveled our launch codes and . . .

He jumped into the water, the hateful thing.

Okay, this meant War! I pried my nose out of the green yucko mud and whirled around to my assistant. "All right, Drover, we're moving into

Stage Two! Get up off the ground and prepare for Ultrasonic Barking!"

"You've got a mud ball on your nose."

"That's your opinion, Drover, and I'm not interested in your opinions. The impointant pork ... the imporkant point ... the important point is that we will surround the pond and unleash a withering barrage of Ultrasonic Barking that will blow the stupid frog right out of the water. Ready? Bark!"

Boy, you should have seen us in action. It was very impressive. Maybe that frog thought he was safe out there in the middle of the pond, but he'd never seen the elite troops of the Security Division in action. The foolish frog.

Drover set up his firing position on the north shore of the pond, while I set up on the south shore. Facing each other across the expanse of green water, we loaded up and began launching round after round of deafening, ear-shattering Ultrasonic Barks.

Minutes passed. Leaves and birds fell from the trees nearby, and one big cottonwood even split in half, no kidding. And out in the middle of the pond, that poor frog ... well, just floated around and didn't actually ...

"All right, Drover!" I yelled over the roar of the battle. "We've given him Stage Two, and now

we're ready to move into Stage Three. Circle the pond and fire off a bark every ten steps. Ready? Let 'im have it!"

The Stage Three Procedure was even more awesome than Stage Two. I mean, it was thunder and lightning, bombs going off, earthquakes and tornadoes! And would you believe that our barking even produced a huge tidal wave? Well, maybe not. But it was some awesome barking. And after a mere two hours ...

We, uh, regrouped on the south shore. Our eyes were wooden, our limp tongues hung out of exhausted mouths, our legs were shaking from the effort of absorbing all the recoil of our barking.

Drover was the first to speak. "He's still out there."

To which I managed to say, "He's still out there, Drover, but we've made our point."

"What was the point? I've already forgotten."

I grabbed several deep breaths, filling my exhausted lungs with a fresh supply of carbon diego. "The point is that we don't allow frogs in our pond. What we couldn't have known was that this frog is too dumb to understand. I think we can notch this one up as a huge moral victory and go on to more important business."

And with that, we stuck out our tongues at the moron frog, gave him monkey ears, and marched away in a triumph, leaving the frog shattered, beaten, and totally humiditated. Humiditied.

Humiliated. There we go. Humiliated.

At this point, you're probably wondering if I've forgotten about the Long-Snouted Road Monster. Not at all. It was a hectic morning, see, and we had a lot of business to take care of. I mean, we're very busy dogs.

And I should probably point out that a lot of your ordinary ranch mutts wouldn't have bothered to do Frogs and Ponds. They would have considered it a waste of their time. Not me, fellers. When it comes to the business of Ranch Security, I figure that no job is too small to be insignificant.

No job is too big to be small.

No job is too small to be . . . phooey.

Where were we? Oh yes. We had just spent the early-morning hours putting down the Frog Rebellion. We had smashed a plot by the United Frog Front to steal Emerald Pond and haul it away to the island of Cowabonga, where they planned to . . . do something with our precious pond.

But we got that stopped just in the nip of the tuck, and as you might expect, the hours and hours of combat had left us exhausted. Yes, we were exhausted but proud, very proud of our team's performance in the heat of battle. Congratulating ourselves on a job well done, we marched away from the smoke and ruins of the battlefield and made our way back to our office on the twelfth floor of the Security Division's Vast Office Complex.

There, we rolled into our gunnysack beds and prepared to indulge ourselves in a few hours of much-needed sleep—sleep that would heal our wounds and prepare us for another dangerous night on Life's front lines. Little did we know or suspect that our period of R&R (Rest and Revitaminization) would be court shot . . . cut short, let us say, or that we would soon be jolted out of our beds by the approach of . . .

Are you sure you're ready for the scary part? I mean, once it starts, there won't be any getting out. No kidding.

Use your own judgment.

CHAPTER THREE

The Invasion of the Road Monster

Okay, there we were, sprawled out on our respective gunnysack beds. I had just closed my weary eyes and had begun to . . . driff oup om the dorking snork of the beetlebomb . . . hot fudgely whickerbill and feathering whiffer piffle . . .

"Hank, do you hear that?"

Had someone just called my name? No. The piffer had merely whiffled in the hot fudgely silence of the—

"Hank? I hear something. Maybe you'd better wake up."

Fighting against the terrible gravitational pull of the hot fudgely silence, I somehow managed to raise my head, and even managed to crank open the outer door of my left eye. And suddenly I saw before me ...

A dog? Or was he a frog in a dog suit? Or a hog in a frog suit, pretending to be a dog? It was very confusing.

"Who are you, and what am I doing here?"

"Well, I'm Drover. Remember me?"

"No. I've never seen me before, so don't try to pretend ..." I cranked open the lid to Eye Number Two, and suddenly a folks came into fakus. It was the folks of a dog ... the face of a dog, let us say, and it came into focus. "Wait a minute, hold everything, pal. I've seen you before."

"Yeah, about five minutes ago. I guess you fell asleep."

"Ha! Not likely." I struggled to my feet and tried to walk a few steps, but it appeared that someone had stolen my legs and had replaced them with four phony legs made of fubb rubber ... fubb roamer ...

I turned a steely gaze on the stranger. "Where are my legs?"

"Well ... I think you're wearing them."

"No, I mean the real ones. These are phony substitutes made of fubb rubber."

"You mean foam rubber?"

"Ah! So you know about this? Okay, pal, who

did it and where are my legs?" I narrowed my eyes and studied the outline of the stranger's face. "Wait a minute, hold everything. Drover? Is that you?"

"Yeah. Hi."

"Thank goodness I've found you. They've stolen my legs! If we don't get them back . . ." All at once, in a rush of insight, I began to realize that . . . uh . . . the things I was saying didn't make a whole lot of sense. I mean, I had just heard myself accusing someone of . . . well, stealing my legs, so to speak, and yet I could see four legs on my . . . uh . . . body.

I took a deep breath of air and blinked my eyes. There in front of me sat Drover, my Assistant Head of Ranch Security. "Drover, how long has this been going on? Don't hold anything back. I must know the truth."

"Well, you were asleep for five minutes. I guess."

"It seemed longer. Weeks. Months. We weren't hiking across the Hot Fudge Mountains?"

"Not me. I don't think so."

"Hmmm. And what about the stolen legs? Did you file a report about . . . why are you staring at me that way? You look like a goofball. If you must stare and look goofy, please go somewhere else." I marched several steps away. "All right, Drover, the pieces of this puzzle are falling into place."

"Oh good, 'cause I'd begun to wonder—"

"Listen carefully. Number one, no one stole my legs. That was a bogus report. Number two, the Hot Fudge Mountains don't exist. And number three, you must swear an oath never to discuss this conversation with anyone outside the Security Division. Do you know why?"

"Well, let me think here."

"Because, Drover"—I dropped my voice to a whisper—"they might get the wrong idea. If they took our words out of context, they might think..."

"...that we're just a couple of dumb dogs?"

"Yes. Right. Exactly. And we must guard against that, Drover, because nothing could be further from the . . ." Suddenly my ears began picking up a sound in the distance. I switched all circuits over to Ear Lift, Right Roll. "Drover, I don't want to alarm you, but I'm picking up an odd sound, coming from somewhere north of us."

"Yeah, I heard the same sound, and that's why I woke you up. It's kind of a roar, isn't it?"

I fine-tuned the Digital Scanneration System and monitored the sound. "Yes, it's a roar, a very unusual kind of roar."

"Yeah, it's kind of a roaring roar."

"Exactly. Yes." I heaved a sigh. "Well, soldier, it appears that we're back on duty. Are you ready for this?"

"Well, I'm kind of tired"—he stood up and began limping around in a circle—"and, boy, this old leg is really giving me fits."

"Never mind the leg, Drover. On this outfit, all roars must be checked out. Stand by to Launch All Dogs!"

Drover whimpered and moaned, but it didn't do him any good. Duty had called, and within seconds, we had launched ourselves into the morning breeze. Once airborne, we set a course that took us around the southeast corner of the yard, then due north toward the county road. Trees, houses, and other objects flew past in blur.

We streaked past the front gate, past the cedar trees in the shelter belt, and then northward toward the mailbox and the county road. It was then that my instruments began picking up . . .

Uh-oh. We've come to the scary part, for you see, what we saw was perhaps the scariest thing I'd ever seen. Do I dare describe it? I'll try.

Okay, hang on. There was this . . . this *thing*, this horrible ugly creature coming down the road in front of us. The first thing I noticed was the sheer size of it: HUGE. I mean, bigger than a pickup, almost as big as a house. It was yellow, and it appeared to be . . .

I know this will sound very strange, but you'll have to trust me here. I mean, I was there and saw it with my own eyes.

It appeared to be some kind of . . . well, huge yellow *face* traveling down the road on six tires. It had two big glassy eyes and a nose . . . a snout . . . a long snout that stuck out in front, and the end of the snout was mounted on . . . tires!

Sound crazy? I understand. It *looked* crazy. I'd never seen anything . . . I mean, that snout was so long, it had to be held up with front tires! And just below the long snout, I saw a wide grinning mouth that appeared to be made of . . . gleaming steel. No kidding.

Oh, and the thing was spewing black smoke from some kind of snorkel or exhaust pipe. And it was roaring. Loud.

Fellers, that was my first glimpse at the Long-Snouted Road Monster, and it was a sight I will never forget. The thing was coming straight toward us, and unless we took some evasive action . . .

"Hit the ditch, Drover!"

All our flight plans, course corrections, calculations, formations . . . everything went out the

window, so to speak, as we scrambled off the road and went rolling into the ditch. And just in the nickering of time. The horrible thing roared past us, leaving us . . . might as well admit it . . . leaving us terrified, gasping for air, and choking on clouds of dust. And diesel fumes.

That was an important clue. Diesel fumes. This hideous monster ran on diesel fuel! Do you see the meaning of this? It meant that this monster, this horrible monster was some kind of . . . well, some kind of *robot machine*, perhaps from outer space! It had been sent to the ranch to . . . we didn't know what dark purpose had brought it to our ranch.

I found myself lying upside down in a patch of tall weeds. A quick scan of the instruments showed that our systems had come through the crash without major damage, which was a big relief and also a big surprise. I mean, we had come very close to being eaten and devoured by . . .

"Drover, where are you? Turn on your emergency beacon."

"No thanks, I'm too scared to eat."

I struggled to my feet, followed the sound of his voice, and found him lying in a clump of ragweed. "Ah, there you are. Thank goodness. How badly are you hurt?"

"Well..."

"Good. There for a second, I was afraid we'd lost you."

"No, I was with me all the time."

"Nice work, son. That was a close call." I looked down the road and saw that the monster was approaching headquarters. "How about it, soldier, can you travel?"

"Well..."

"Great. Let's move out. We must warn the house that a Long-Snouted Road Monster is on the loose."

"Gosh, I thought it was a road grader."

"Road grader? Ha. We should be so lucky. No, Graver, what we just witnessed was no rade groder."

"Drover. My name's Drover."

I glared at the runt. "Why are you telling me your name? I know your name."

"Yeah, but you called me ... I think you called me Radegroder."

"I did *not* call you Radegroder. I said ... never mind, Groder, we've got work to do. Let's move out!"

"My name's Drover."

Battered and wounded though we were, we made our way down the road to check this thing out.

CHAPTER FOUR

A Terrible
Bloody Battle

I noticed that Drover was limping pretty badly. "How's the leg, son?"

"Terrible. The pain's about to kill me, and it hurt my feelings that you called me . . . Groder."

"I did *not* call you . . . okay, maybe I did. But it was a simple mistake, made in a moment of great stress and tension. After all, we had just been attacked by that huge monster."

"Yeah, but I still say it's a road grader."

"Drover, please. It's not a road grader. Do you know why?" He opened his mouth to answer, but I plunged on with my lecture, knowing that he had nothing important to say. "Number one, county employees grade county roads. Number two, this little piece of a road going down to headquarters is a private road, not a county road."

"Yeah, but—"

"Number three, every road grader has a driver, Drover, whereas your Long-Snouted Monsters have no driver. Did you see a driver in that thing?"

"Yeah, as a matter of fact—"

"See? No driver, no grader. And number four, if that had actually been a road grader, don't you suppose the Head of Ranch Security would have noticed it right away?"

"Well—"

"Drover, you're arguing a hopeless case. I've given you four excellent reasons why you're wrong about this, and you've offered no evidence, not one shred of evidence, to the contrary."

"Yeah, 'cause you keep butting in."

I stopped in the middle of the road and stared at him with . . . well, hurt and amazement in my eyes. "Butting in? Is that the thanks I get for trying to improve your mind? For trying to keep you from making a spectacle of yourself? Drover, I can't tell you how deeply this wounds me."

"Yeah, but I know it was a road grader, 'cause I saw the driver inside the cab, and it had 'John Deere' written on the side."

"Please stop yelling at me."

"Well, you never listen."

I heaved a weary sigh and shook my head. This was a very sad moment for the Security Division. We had important work to do, but it would have to wait until I had given Drover his Lesson for the Day.

I marched back and forth in front of him. "Drover, we've discussed spies and monsters, right? They're clever beyond our wildest dreams, and when they invade our ranch, do you suppose they waltz in, dressed as spies and monsters? No. They always come disguised as something else."

"You mean . . ."

"Yes, Drover. It's the old Road Grader Disguise—a layer of yellow paint and a phony John Deere sign. These monsters aren't stupid. Do you think they'd come in here looking like monsters? Ha. You don't know these guys the way I know them."

He plopped down and started scratching his ear. "You mean . . ."

"At this point, we don't know who he is, Drover, or who sent him onto our ranch, but it looks very suspicious, doesn't it? And I wish you wouldn't scratch in public. If someone saw us here, he might think we were just goofing off."

"Boy, that would be wrong. What'll we do now?"

I narrowed my eyes and studied the layout of ranch headquarters. "We're going in, son. Lock and load. This could get us into some serious combat."

"Oh, my leg!"

And with that, we arranged ourselves into Attack Formation and began creeping down the road toward headquarters. Our objective on this mission was to . . . well, we had two objectives, actually.

The first was to warn our friends at the house that a dangerous, possibly deadly Robot Space Monster had perpetrated our prepatory . . . had penetrated our territory, shall we say. And our second objective—if we were lucky enough to survive the first—was to engage the enemy in face-to-face, hand-to-hand combat. In other words, it was our job to clear the ranch of all monsters.

Yes, it was a bold plan, a dangerous plan. I knew that our odds of surviving the mission weren't so great, but . . . well, when I signed on as Head of Ranch Security, I knew the job would be no bed of nails.

No bed of rose petals.

I knew it would be no flower bed.

I knew the bed would be full of . . .

Wait! Hold everything! "Eternal bedsprings."

Remember that? Was this some kind of clue that might blow the case wide open?

No. It meant nothing. Forget it.

This promised to be a very dangerous mission, is the point, and it would have nothing to do with beds or rosebushes. I knew there was a high risk that we would never . . . well, never come back alive, might as well blurt it out.

But that's what cowdogs do. We live our lives as long as we can, and then we go down fighting for the ranch.

Was I nervous? Scared? Not even a little . . . okay, maybe I was just a tad nervous, maybe even scared. Who wouldn't have been scared? You saw that horrible monster, right? It was not only enormous and disguised as a road grader, but it was also wearing a coat of *armored steel plate*. Could our Barkolasers penetrate that steel plating? Would our Fang Missiles be strong enough to disable the huge tires?

Those were the questions that filled my mind as I struggled to prepare myself for the coming battle. Unfortunately, we had no answers, and questions that have no answers are like . . . something.

Anyways, we crept forward, moving on paws that made not a sound. Thirty liters north of the house, I halted the column. Typically, Drover ran into me, because he wasn't paying attention. He does it every time.

I scouted the terrapin ahead . . . the terrain, shall we say. Terrapins are turtles, don't you see, and have nothing to do with . . . never mind. I scouted the so forth and suddenly realized that the Road Monster hadn't gone to the house, as you might have expected, but had gone instead to the machine shed.

Do you see the meaning of this? I didn't. I found it confusing. I mean, why would a monster . . . once again, we didn't have any answers, but we would soon find out. Since we were observing Strict Radio Silence, I gave Drover hand signals to indicate that we would now move toward the machine shed. He . . .

You won't believe this. I guess the little stupe thought I was . . . well, waving at him or something, so he grinned and waved back.

I dropped my voice to a whisper. "What are you doing?"

"Well, I thought . . . were you waving at me?"

"No, I was not. I was giving you *secret hand signals.*"

"I'll be derned. What did they mean?"

"Drover, if I have to tell you what they mean,

there's no point in giving them. I'll flash the signals one more time, and please try to concentrate."

I flashed him the signals again. He rolled his eyes and appeared to be concentrating. "Well, let's see here. You said . . . it's time for a nice long nap?"

The air hissed out of my lungs. My eyelids sank. All at once, I felt as though I had been buried under a mountain of . . . "Drover, just forget the hand signals. We're moving our troops down to the machine shed. Prepare for combat."

"You know, Hank, this old leg—"

"Let's go, soldier. Be brave, and don't hold anything back for tomorrow."

"Help!"

And with that, we went charging down the hill. I took the lead, of course, and hoped that Drover would be right behind me, guarding our rears and flanks. (As you'll soon find out, he wasn't). I burst upon the scene and laid down a withering barrage of Spray Barking, which is the technique we use when . . . well, when we're not exactly sure what or whom we're barking at.

It was your classic battlefield situation—the air filled with smoke and dust, bombs going off all around us, the deafening roar of gunfire, soldiers and enemy agents yelling and running in all directions, the whine of incoming mortar shells overhead ... boy, what a scene!

Up ahead of us, through the dust and smoke, I saw the hulking Road Monster. It was standing ... or sitting, it was hard to say which ... it was standing or sitting right in front of the machine shed, preparing to ... we didn't know what it was doing. Maybe it had gotten the crazy idea that it could bust into the machine shed and steal all our dog food, or maybe it planned to ... well, eat tools or something.

Over the sounds of battle, I yelled, "Okay, Drover, there he is! Go for the tires! Let's see if we can—"

"You know, Hank, that thing's bigger than I thought and—"

ZOOM! You won't believe this. I heard a rush of wind and saw a streak of white, and caught a glimpse of my assistant as he scampered into the machine shed.

"Drover, get yourself out here and stand your ground! That is a direct order!"

But it was already too late. The little weenie had left me alone on the field of battle, and now I had to ... gulp ... face the awful Road Monster without help or backup or ...

HUH?

Three men? Standing in front of the machine shed doors? Grinning? Who were those guys, and where had they ...

I went to Full Air Brakes and shut everything down. Through the clouds of smoke and dust, I saw ...

Okay, we can call off the Code Three. Just relax for a minute while we ... you probably thought we were going into a serious combat situation against a huge Road Monster, right? Ha-ha. There for a second or two, I'd thought so myself. I mean, in the heat of battle, we sometimes get faulty readings on our ... when that huge thing had been coming straight at us, it had looked very much like a huge enormous ...

You're really going to be surprised when I tell you that it was just ... ha-ha ... just an ordinary old *road grader*. No kidding. Just an ordinary yellow John Deere road grader that belonged to the county, so ... uh ... no big deal.

And those three strange men? Ha-ha. Again, no problem. Right away, I recognized Slim and Loper, the two cowboys on our outfit, and the third guy ... well, we had reason to suppose that he might be ...

This is very embarrassing. Let's just skip it. I refuse to say another word about it.

CHAPTER FIVE

Okay, It Was a Road Grader

Oh, what the heck, I guess it wouldn't hurt to ... he was the driver, see. The operator. The county employee who, uh, drove the machine. The grader.

Every grader has a driver, don't you see, and his name was Maurice. He often graded our roads. I mean, I recognized him right away: tall and skinny, wore a pair of blue overalls and an old felt cowboy hat pulled down to his ears. I'd barked at him a few times on the county road and knew he was a pretty good feller, a retired cowboy, in fact, so ...

Ha-ha. So what we had here was no big deal at all, just a gathering of friends and neighbors who seemed to be laughing at my ... all of a

40

sudden, I felt that I had become the center of everyone's attention, shall we say, and yes, I did feel a bit exposed and embarrassed.

They were staring at me. And grinning.

Maurice: "Do you ever wonder what goes through a dog's mind?"

Slim: "I used to, but then I figured out that Hank ain't got one. See, the day they was passing out brains, Hank thought they said *trains* and he didn't order one."

There! You see how they act? Everything's a big joke. Make one little mistake around here and ... phooey.

Well, I had more important things to do than stand there, listening to their idle chatter, so I did what any normal American dog would have done. Holding my head at a proud angle, I marched over to one of the back tires and gave it a squirt of Secret Encoding Fluid. That way, if this turned out to be some kind of trick ...

Maurice: "Do you boys charge for the tire wash?"

Slim: "First tire's free. After that, we charge a buck and a half."

They got a big chuckle out of that. I didn't see the humor of it myself. I mean, a guy devotes his whole life to protecting the ranch and taking care of business, but it's never enough to satisfy the Small Minds of this world.

Fine. I didn't need their approval. Sometimes we dogs have to ignore everything the humans say around here, knowing in our deepest hearts . . .

Loper: "Boys, I hate to break up the fun, but we've got work to do. What size bolt do you need, Maurice?"

Well, what do you know? At that moment, a small miracle occurred. They stopped chattering and making stale jokes, and went into the machine shed to do something constructive for a change—find a three-quarter-inch bolt for Maurice's grader.

See, that's why Maurice had come into head-quarters—he'd broken a bolt on the grader blade, and he'd stopped to see if we had a spare. I had suspected that all along, no kidding. I mean, when we first saw that thing coming down the road, I said, "Drover, that grader has a broken bolt where the blade connects to the frame."

Didn't I say that? Maybe I didn't actually say it out loud, but I *noticed* the broken bolt, no kidding, and made a mental note to . . .

When the Loafers and Jokers cleared the area and went slouching into the machine shed, the air was suddenly filled with the sounds of clanging and banging as they began pouring out the contents of fifteen coffee cans onto the workbench.

Why coffee cans? Because that's where Loper and Slim stored all the ranch's inventory of bolts, nuts, screws, washers, fasteners, and cotter pins. They had fifteen old coffee cans lined up on the back of the workbench, and every one of 'em was crammed full of bolts and stuff.

That was their "system" for organizing the spare parts. They tossed any bolt or screw into any can so that when they needed one, they had to go through every can every time. It's called the Cowboy Way, which is just another name for sloppy management.

Now, if they'd asked *my* opinion . . . but let's don't get into that. It would serve no purpose and would merely open old wounds. I mean, who am I? Just a dumb dog who barks at road graders, but let me point out that no dog in history has ever made such a mess of . . . oh well.

Where were we? Oh yes, crashing and banging in the machine shed. The Loafers and Scoffers had finally left me alone in front of the machine shed, and I was about to proceed with the Trademarking of Tires Procedure, when suddenly, I heard a sound above me. At first I thought it was a voice, but then . . .

Well, it *was* a voice, and it said, "Hello down there. What you doing?"

I swept my gaze around the area in front of the shed and saw nothing. Then I remembered an important clue: The sound had seemed to come from *above*. Remember? So I lifted my eyes to the cab of the ... well, of the stupid road grader that had tried its best to run over the entire Security Division, and there I saw ...

A dog.

No kidding, it was a dog, but what was a dog doing in the cab of a county road grader? At that point, we had no answer to that crucial question, but right away we scanned in a description of the mutt and sent it straight to Data Control.

Would you care to take a peek? I guess it wouldn't hurt anything.

Description of Unidentified
Dog on Ranch
Case #49596-B12-H2O

Color: reddish brown, black spot around
left eye.

Hair Texture: short.

Tail: long and sticklike.

Breed: mixed, Heinz 57; this guy is a
mutt.

Eyes: brown and goofy.

IQ: pretty low, judging by the expression on his face.

Reason for Being on the Ranch: unknown at this point, but we'll find out.

End of File

Pretty impressive, huh? You bet. You'll notice that the Security Division doesn't keep its information in coffee cans.

Anyways, we had us an unidentified mutt on the ranch, and I went right to work. First thing, I bristled the hair on the back of my neck and went into a barking program that we call "You Don't Belong Here." The idea behind this routine is to give the other guy such a ferocious blast of barking that he'll either run away or cringe in fear. See, we've found that when we hit 'em hard right away, they're not likely to fight back, bark back, or mouth off.

(That's pretty hard to say, isn't it? Try it three times, real fast: *fight back, bark back, or mouth off*. Pretty tough).

I barked and barked, and we're talking about deep ferocious barks that should have sent him running for cover. I mean, it was a great presentation, but for some reason the mutt just sat there and ... well, grinned down at me. When I paused to refill my tanks with air, he said, in a high-pitched squeaky voice, "Hey down there, who are you barking at?"

I grabbed a deep breath. "I'm barking at *you*, fella. Who do you think?"

"Well, I wondered. I didn't see anybody else around. But why would you be barking at me?"

"I'm barking at you because you're on my ranch, and because you don't have permission to be on my ranch. It's called trespassing, and we get pretty serious about trespassers."

"Oh-h-h, I see now. I thought maybe you were mad 'cause my road grader's better than your road grader."

I beamed him an ice pick glare. "Your road grader's better than mine? Is that what you just said?"

He grinned and nodded. "Yep. See, a lot of dogs are jealous 'cause I get to ride in a road grader and they don't. They get mad and bark."

I rolled my eyes and looked away. What kind of goofball was this guy? Imagine him thinking that I might be jealous of his ...

"For your information, pal, your road grader *isn't* better than mine."

His ears jumped. "You've got one, too?"

"Sure. Hey, I'm Head of Ranch Security."

"Aw heck. What kind of grader do you have?"

"Oh, the...uh...the good kind, the best money can buy. In fact, I've got three of 'em."

His eyes grew wide. "You've got three road graders?"

"Four, actually. We bought a new one last week."

"Wow! Where are they?"

"They're, uh, parked in the barn."

"This barn?"

"No, they're parked in the, uh, road grader barn. See, we've got a special barn for all our graders."

"Wow. Can I look at 'em?"

"I'm afraid not. It's a secured area, and it's not open to the public. Sorry."

He shook his head in amazement. "Wow. I never met a dog that had *four road graders*."

"Well, now you have. I guess this is your lucky day. But the point is that your road grader isn't better than mine, so we can move along to other matters. What else can you do?"

He seemed a little more humble now. "Well, gosh, let me think. I guard baby chicks."

"Baby chicks? You guard baby chicks? Is that what you said?"

He grinned. "Yep, and I'm pretty good at it, too. How about yourself?"

"Fine, thanks."

"No, I mean, can you guard baby chicks? See, Maurice's wife ... Betty's her name ... Betty raises baby chickens and sells 'em, and I have to guard 'em. It's my job."

I rolled my eyes and walked a few steps away. "What did you say your name was?"

"Well ... I didn't say. It's Dixie."

"Okay, Dipsy, let me lay a couple of things out for you. Number one, I'm a cowdog. Number two, I'm Head of Ranch Security."

"Aw! No fooling?"

"I'm not finished. Number three, a top-of-the-line, blue-ribbon cowdog would never waste his time guarding a bunch of sniveling little chickens."

Dipsy cocked his head to the side. "Yeah, but our chickies don't snivel. They cheep."

"Well, if they're so cheap, maybe you should raise the price."

He blinked his eyes and scowled. "No, what I said was, they *cheep*. You know, *cheep-cheep*. That's what they say. That's how they talk."

"Oh. Yes, of course. I, uh, thought . . . so your chickens cheep?"

"No, the chickens cluck, the big 'uns do. The

chickies cheep. They're little bitty fellers, see, and they can't cluck, so they cheep. Their mommies cluck. You don't know much about chickens, do you?"

I paced over to the cab and beamed him a stern glare. "Just for your information, pal, we have chickens on this ranch, and I know just about everything there is to know about chickens."

Dipsy cut his eyes from side to side and gave me a sly grin. "You ever eat one?"

Suddenly, my tongue shot out and I found myself . . . uh . . . licking my chops, shall we say. "I'm shocked that you would even . . . *slurp* . . . suggest such a thing. No, absolutely . . . *slurp* . . . not."

"Heh. I did, once. Best meal I ever had. It tasted just like chicken, but it got me in a world of trouble." He narrowed his eyes. "How come you're drooling at the mouth?"

"Me? I'm not . . ." I found it necessary to, uh, turn away from him. "For your inslurpation, I'm not drooling at the mouth, and could we change the slurpish?"

"Okay, sure, but I thought you were drooling at the mouth or something."

"No. You have no evidence of that and you can't prove a thing. Furthermore, I'm so outraged that I'm going to end this converslurption. I've never been so inslurpled. Good-bye!"

And with that, I whirled to the right and marched away from the cad. The very idea! Him, coming onto my ranch and making up lies and half-truths about the Head of Ranch Slurpurity! Just for that, he could enjoy his own boring company and sit alone in his slummy little road grader.

Filled with rage and righteous anger, I stormed away and met Little Alfred, just as he was coming up the hill from the house.

CHAPTER SIX

Pete Steals Food from Hungry Children

A lfred was dressed in his usual little boy clothes—striped overalls, T-shirt, little black boots, and a cowboy straw hat. And in his right hand ... left hand ... it doesn't matter ... in one of his hands, either the right or the left, he carried ...

My goodness, what was that? I caught the smell of it right away ... sniff, sniff ... and it bore a strong resemblance to ... uh ... breakfast sausage.

Breakfast sausage! Wow.

Have we discussed breakfast sausage? Maybe

not. We're talking about the kind that comes in links. What do they call them? Little Piggies or something like that. It doesn't matter. The point is that I, uh, have a very strong reaction every time I'm exposed to those . . . lick, slurp . . . Little Piggie Sausages.

The sudden appearance of Little Piggie Sausage Waves in the atmosphere causes my ears to jump, my eyes to pop open, my front feet to move up and down, my tail to switch into Wild Excited Patterns of Wagging, and my mouth to . . . well, water like crazy.

Can we pause here for me to make a confession? Might as well get it over with.

I'm nuts about Little Piggie Sausages! I love 'em! I'd rather eat a Little Piggie Sausage than anything else in the whole world!

There, I've said it. It's out in the open, and my confession will help smooth the way for, uh, what follows, shall we say, for you see . . .

It happened suddenly. I wasn't expecting it. I hadn't planned it. It just . . .

See, Alfred was holding that yummy thing in his hand . . . actually, between his thumb and first finger . . . he was holding it up in the air, don't you know, and kind of waving it around, and maybe he didn't notice that my head was moving back and forth, exactly in time with the luscious sausage.

My mouth continued to water. My ears jumped. I moved my front paws up and down, and by this time my tail was thrashing the air in crazy patterns that . . . slurp, slurp . . . were so strong and powerful that they made it hard for me to keep my balance.

In other words, the wave patterns coming off that Little Piggie Sausage were creating a huge disturbance in the force field of my . . .

As I've already said, I hadn't planned anything. Nothing at all. I was just standing there, minding my own biscuits . . . business, I guess it should be . . . minding my own business, and Alfred was holding up the sausage and then . . .

Well, he turned his head away for just an instant. Was that my fault? No, I'd had nothing to do with it. I think he was looking back at the cat, but the point, the crucial point, is that just for a second, he looked away and . . .

. . . and there was that yummy sausage, all alone and just sitting there in his fingers!

You've seen pictures of the Statue of Liberty, right? She's standing there in the middle of a big lake and holding up her right hand, and she's

clasping a link of Little Piggie Sausage. No kidding. You didn't know that? It's true, honest.

She's holding up the sausage for all the world to see, and she says, "Give me your tired, your hungry!" Do you see the meaning of this? It means...

Hang on, this gets kind of emotional.

It means that Lady Liberty is calling hungry dogs from all over the world to come to America's shores and eat sausage! Hungry dogs from Texas and Canada Dry and Bovina, Mesopotamia, and Pottawatami, Italy, and France and . . . everywhere.

She's calling them...us...to come and share her bounty of yummy sausage, and all at once I realized that Little Alfred looked exactly like the Statue of Liberty and...

SNARF!

. . . and all at once and before my very eyes, the, uh, sausage just . . . vanished.

Alfred's eyes came around and he stared at his thumb and finger where the, uh, Little Piggie Sausage had once...resided, shall we say. Where it had been only moments before.

His puzzled gaze drifted around to . . . well, to ME, you might say, and I gave him a big good morning smile, as if to say, "Oh. Hi. Nice day, huh?"

He stared at his empty hand. "Where'd my sausage go?"

Sausage? Had he . . . ? Oh yes, of course, the sausage. Remember that Little Piggie Sausage? He'd been holding it in his hand, and apparently a sudden gust of wind had . . . the wind was coming up, see, and you know this Texas wind. Boy, if you're not careful, it'll blow things right out of your . . .

He scowled and looked down at the ground. Good thinking. If the wind had blown the sausage out of his hand, it probably would have fallen to the ground. I leaped to my feet and rushed to the scene of the, uh, accident. I lowered my nose to the ground and activated our Emergency Locator Program. We use it for special deals, anytime something gets lost—you know, missing children, important pieces of evidence, articles of clothing, stuff like that.

I switched on the ELP and proceeded to sniff out the whole area around his feet. By George, if the boy's sausage had fallen to the ground, we were going to find it, even if it took days or weeks!

These kids need a good nourishing breakfast.

I searched and searched, sniffed and sniffed, but after searching and sniffing for hours and hours . . . okay, a minute or two . . . I came up with nothing, not even a trace of the Elusive Sausage. My heart was almost broken. The poor lad! I lifted my head and beamed him a look of Deepest Sadness.

"Alfred, it grieves me deeply to tell you this, but the sausage has disappeared without a trace. I'm sorry."

I went to Slow and Caring Wags on the tail section, just to let him know that . . . well, even though my heart was broken, my tail still worked.

That doesn't sound right. I wanted him to know, through wags and tragic expressions on my facial situation, that my heart was broken over this deal.

I studied his face to see if my presentation was . . . uh . . . selling. I held my breath.

His eyes narrowed into slits. "Hankie, did you eat my sausage?"

Who? Me? Eat his . . . hey, who had rushed to the scene of the tragedy to share his pain and search for the missing sausage? Me! And now he was wondering if I had . . .

Just then, the cat came slithering into the picture—purring and rubbing and wearing that sniveling grin that drives me nuts. It was Pete, of course, Pete the Barncat who never spends any time in the barn because he's too busy loafing in the iris patch and trying to mooch scraps.

Have we discussed Pete? I don't like him, never have, but there he was, rubbing on Alfred's ankles and grinning. All at once, his eyes popped open and he lifted his nose in the air. "My goodness, Hankie, I smell something good. Could it be . . . sausage?"

I cut my eyes from side to side. Suddenly a plan began to take shape in the vast caverns of my mind. Or to put it another way, it suddenly occurred to me that one of the many things I didn't like about Pete was that he was just the kind of creep who would *steal sausage from a hungry child*.

Did you catch the clues? Maybe not, so let's do a quick review.

1. Cat walks up.

2. Out of the blue, for no reason whatever, cat says something about sausage.

3. Kid is looking for missing sausage.

Do you get it now? All at once all the pieces of this mysterious puzzle began falling into place. I turned my eyes upon my dearest pal, Little Alfred, and went to the Urgent Message routine on the tail section, which consists of a slow, circular, counterclockwise motion. Then, with the Urgent Message program still running, I pointed my nose directly at the cat.

"Alfred, I'm shocked that you would accuse me of terrible crimes, but never mind. The culprit just walked up. I won't mention any names, but I think it was . . . PETE."

Alfred looked deeply into my . . . yikes . . . eyes, but then . . . heh-heh . . . he turned his gaze upon the cat, the sneaking cheating little hickocrip of a cat, and a dark frown began to form upon his face. Heh-heh.

And he said, "Pete, did you eat my sausage? You did, you naughty cat, and I don't wike you anymore!"

And with that, he aimed a boot at Kitty's hinelary region and, heh-heh, gave him the kick he so richly deserved for being all the things he was.

Tee-hee! Ho-ho, ha-ha, hee-hee!

Oh, justice! Oh, truth and honor! I loved it! Kitty was shocked beyond recognition. I mean, he never saw it coming. He hissed and squealed, made a short flight through the air, and scurried away, throwing daggerish looks back at me.

Did I care about his daggerish looks? Heck no. The little pest had been caught in the act of robbing breakfast from hungry children, and he'd gotten just what he deserved.

As he slithered away to the iris patch, he managed to hiss a few hateful words to me. "Very funny, Hankie. I'll remember this."

"You do that, Kitty. Remember what happens to cats who sneak and steal and rob from innocent children! I'm shocked, Pete, shocked beyond words."

Told him, huh? You bet.

CHAPTER SEVEN

I Prescribe a Cure
for Drover's Malady

Okay, maybe it was mean of me to eat the sausage and blame the cat, but I must point out that Little Alfred caused the whole thing with his careless behavior. If he didn't want his poor hungry dog to snarf down the sausage, he should have . . . I don't know, put it in his pocket or something.

And besides, who cares if a cat gets in trouble once in a while? Cats need to be humbled, don't forget that, and Pete needed it even more than most.

Well, Little Alfred left the scene of the crime and wandered over to look at the road grader whilst I enjoyed the aftertaste of the Sausage of

My Dreams. But suddenly I found myself looking into the vast emptiness of Drover's eyes.

"Why are you staring at me?"

"Well...you told a fib and got Pete in trouble. I'm kind of shocked."

"I'm sorry."

"Are you really sorry?"

"No. Find something to do besides stare at me."

He continued staring at me. "And you didn't share the sausage with me. That really hurts."

"Too bad. Stop staring and move your carcass."

"What about the rest of me?"

"Your carcass is the sum total of everything you are, Drover. Move it."

"Yeah, but what about my mind? My personality? The real me, deep inside? If I move the carcass, I'll have to move the rest of it, too."

Was he trying to be funny? It was hard to tell. "Drover, your mind is so tiny, and your personality so shallow and empty, they hardly take up any space. Therefore, as I've already said, your carcass is the sum totality of your being."

"I ate a bean once. Mom said it would sprout in my stomach and the vines would grow out my ears."

"This is boring me, Drover."

"But you know what? It grew out my nose."

I stared at the runt. "Wait a minute. Are you saying that you ate a bean and it sprouted and grew out your nose? I find that very hard to believe."

"Yeah, but it's true. It was big and green."

"Well, maybe it wasn't a bean sprout. Maybe it was some kind of disgusting discharge from your nosalary region. Had you considered that?"

"Well, by doze geds stobbed ub all the tibe. Baby thad was id."

"Of course that was it. In the history of the world, there has never been a single case of a bean sprouting in a dog's stomach and growing out his ... Drover, why are we discussing beans in the first place? Deep in my heart, I really don't care about the subject."

"Yeah, me neither, and I don't know beans about 'em anyway."

"Exactly my point. If you knew beans about beans, you'd know that they can't possibly—"

"I ate a kernel of corn one time, too."

This got my attention. "Wait a minute, hold it. Colonel Corn? Who is he and why didn't you tell me about him sooner?"

"Well . . . I didn't think you'd care. You don't care about beans."

"I don't care about beans, Drover, and for very good reason. There's a huge difference between beans and colonels."

"Yeah, I guess a bean is just a seed."

"Exactly, whereas a colonel is a high-ranking officer, perhaps even an enemy spy. Now, out with it. Details, facts. Is there more to this Colonel Corn business?"

The little mutt seemed to be looking guilty about something. He swallowed hard and glanced around. "Well, maybe one thing."

"See? I knew it. There's always one more thing. Out with it!"

"Well, it was . . . it was . . ."

"Yes, yes?"

"It was . . . popcorn."

That word hung in the air between us for a long moment of heartbeats. "What?"

"Popcorn."

"I heard what you said, Drover, but I'm finding it hard to fit 'popcorn' into your description of a high-ranking member of the Enemy's military intelligence unit—who, by the way, might very well be the same guy who ordered the Road Grader Invasion of our ranch. Had you thought of that?"

"Not really."

"Hurry up. Where did you see this Colonel Corn?"

"Well . . . in a paper sack."

"Aha! Paper sack! This is a new one." I began pacing, as I often do when these cases take a new and puzzling twist. "It's obviously some kind of disguise. He wore the bag over his head, right? It was some kind of hood or mask. Okay, we're cooking now, son. Continue."

"Well, Sally May cooked some kernels of popcorn and put 'em in a paper sack, and Little Alfred was eating the popcorn and he gave me a bite."

I stopped in my tracks and turned slowly around. "What are we talking about?"

"Well . . . I'm not sure. Popcorn, I think."

"What about this . . . this mysterious colonel?"

"Well, it was a mysterious kernel of popcorn. I guess."

The air hissed out of my lungs. Suddenly my head seemed full of fog. Or feathers. I marched a few steps away and gazed up at the sky. "Drover, has it ever occurred to you that one of us might be . . . unbalanced?"

"Sometimes I get dizzy when I turn around. Could that be it?"

"No, it's worse than that. I often find myself

feeling dizzy when I talk to you. It's almost as though..." I paused to search for the right words. "It's almost as though our conversations are meaningless. Nonsense. They just . . . go in circles. Do you ever get that feeling?"

He wadded up his mouth and squinted one eye. "Well, let me think. No, I kind of enjoy—"

"Never mind." I marched over to him. "Skip it. I'm sorry I asked. This loony conversation will be stricken from the record. If anyone asks about Colonel Corn, we'll say we never heard of him. The world must never know what we discuss behind closed doors."

Drover glanced around. "Okay, but where's the door?"

I could feel my eyes bulging out of my head. "There isn't a door, you meathead! Therefore, the world must never know what we *don't* discuss behind closed doors. Is that plain enough?"

"You never hear about a kernel of beans."

"Hush! Not another word! What were we discussing before you led us off in meaningless circles?"

There was a long silence as Drover searched the thimble of his mind. Then his eyes popped open. "Oh yeah, I remember now. You stole Little Alfred's sausage and didn't give me a bite, and now I feel terrible. I wanted some sausage!"

I marched over to him and laid a paw on his shoulder. "You really feel bad about this, don't you?"

"Awful. I wanted that sausage more than anything in the whole world."

"Drover, this problem of yours is called Sausage Lust. It's a serious condition that strikes dogs and renders them worthless."

"I'll be derned. That fits."

"It does. But I think I can help you through this time of loss and sorrow."

His eyes lit up. "Really? No fooling?"

"Yes. For you see, there is a cure for Sausage Lust, but you have to follow instructions and do exactly as I say."

He was hopping up and down. "Oh, sure, I'll do anything to get my life back."

"Good. Stop hopping around and listen. I'm going to prescribe a cure." He sat down and listened. "Go directly to your room and sit on a sticker for thirty minutes."

"A sticker?"

"Exactly. You see, Drover, the root of the heart of the core of your problem is that you have no self-control."

"Yeah, but—"

"You seem to crave things you can't have."

"Yeah, but—"

"Sitting on a sticker will develop your powers of self-control. After thirty minutes of sticker-sitting, you will no longer be tormented by these feelings of Sausage Lust."

"Yeah, 'cause it'll hurt like crazy."

"Pain, Drover, is the fire that purifies the mind."

He blinked his eyes in wonder. "I'll be derned. But . . . wait a second. You're the one who ate the sausage. All I did was wish for it. How come you don't have to sit on a sticker?"

"Drover, we all have problems and failings, but yours and mine aren't the same. Your problem is greed and selfishness. Mine was mere hunger. Now run along. Once you've spent an hour feeling bad, you'll feel much better."

"I thought you said thirty minutes."

"We've increased your medication. This is worse than I thought. Now run along."

He walked away, shaking his head and mumbling to himself. As I watched him making his way down to the gas tanks, I must admit that I felt a glow of pride and satisfaction. I mean, there are some parts of this job that are just dull routine, but when you can actually reach out and touch the life of another dog . . . help him see that he's been living a wasted life, that he's been consumed with lowly impulses of greed and so forth . . .

Hey, it doesn't get much better than that.

To celebrate this great turnaround in Drover's life experience, I skipped up to the machine shed and indulged myself in a few bites of Co-op dog food. I mean, let's face it: Little Piggie Sausage is great stuff, but one of them doesn't go very far.

Don't forget the wise old saying: "This Little Piggie went to market; this Little Piggie stayed home; this Little Piggie ate roast beef, but Hankie only got to eat one."

CHAPTER EIGHT

Alfred Decides to Raise Baby Chicks

I know that we've discussed Co-op dog food, so we needn't go into great detail in describing it. It comes in a fifty-pound sack. That should tell you a lot right there.

You know what comes in fifty-pound sacks? Cement, masonry sand, whole potatoes, uncooked onions, horse feed, and deer corn. None of those items is fit to eat.

Things that are fit to eat come in small packages, such as your steaks, your chops, your roasts, your bacon, and your Little Piggie Sausages. We dogs are never offered food items that come in small packages. Is that fair? No, but that's the way life is lived out here in the Real World.

Our primary ration, Co-op Brand Dry Dog

Food, is purchased at the Co-op Feed Store, where it sits in a big echoing warehouse, in a stack of sacks five feet tall and five feet wide. Several times each month, Slim visits the feed store, strolls into the warehouse, and perhaps notices sparrows fluttering around in the rafters. The birds are not supposed to be there but they are, and you can guess what they leave on the sacks below.

Slim pulls a rumpled piece of paper out of his pocket, squints at the items scrawled on it, and calls out the order to a sleepy-eyed laborer who has been rousted from his afternoon nap.

"Jerry, I'll take four horse feed, ten stock salt, two whole corn, and five sand-mix cement. Oh, and one dog food."

The laborer yawns. "Active or Semi-active?"

"Pardon?"

"What do the dogs do? Hunt, work . . . ?"

This provokes a laugh. "They sleep and bark. Do you have a Sleep and Bark ration?"

"Nope. Active or Semi-active."

"Semi."

And the laborer shuffles through the dusty warehouse, loading sacks onto a two-wheel dolly. He pushes the dolly to the loading dock and heaves the sacks into the back of the ranch pickup.

Does this sound appetizing? Does it make you want to rush up to the machine shed and devour a bowl of Co-op dog food kernels? Oh, and don't forget that we don't even have a respectable dog bowl. They put our food in an overturned Ford hubcap.

Now I ask you this. If the people on this outfit went out to eat at a restaurant, would they sit down in a big warehouse with sparrows swooping around overhead, and order something that came out of a fifty-pound sack? Oh no. But when it comes to their dogs . . .

Oh well. There's no sense in getting worked up over the injustice in the world.

I went to the dog bowl, which was heaped high with yellowish kernels, and gave it several sniffs. One sniff would have been enough to inform me that my dreams of Little Piggie Sausage had vanished into thinnest air, gone forever like dewdrops on the morning spring.

Dewdrops in the springtime on blades of . . .

Spring drops of dew on the morning . . .

Phooey.

The sausage was gone, is the point. I loaded my mouth with dry tasteless kernels and went straight into the Crusher Program.

When we're running the CP, there is a period

of fifteen to thirty seconds when we have to listen to all the noise in the Crusher Compartment. (Ordinary dogs sometimes call it "the mouth.") Crack! Snap! Crunch! It's very loud. If you happen to have a headache, it makes you think that you have a jackhammer inside your head.

Oh well. Limestone rocks or tree bark might taste worse, and might even be harder to chew. I paused a moment to be thankful for Co-op Brand Semi-active Dry Dog Food kernels.

As I was grinding up my morning nourishment... oh, and speaking of nourishment, did you happen to notice that the cowboys buy the *cheaper* brand of dog food? Maybe you missed that. Semi-active is cheaper than Active, and that's why they buy it. It has nothing to do with the schedules or work routines of the Security Division. Semi-active is cheaper, period.

Where were we? Oh yes. As I was laboring to grind up and crush my morning so forth, three adult males and one boy strolled out of the machine shed. I looked up from my work and recognized Slim, Loper, and Maurice (the adult males), and Little Alfred (the boy). Did I care? No. I was busy, grinding rocks of dog food and trying to forget that they weren't sausage links.

Maurice said, "Well, thanks for the bolt. That saved me a trip back to town. Oh, by the way, I'm going to be the poultry superintendent at the county fair this year. That boy ought to show some chickens. It's a good wholesome project for these kids."

Loper looked down at Little Alfred. "What do you say, young'un? Would you like to show chickens at the fair?"

Alfred nodded. "Sure! Maybe I could win a wibbon."

Loper turned back to Maurice. "Sounds like you've started something." He gestured toward several hens pecking grasshoppers in front of the chicken house. "Would those do?"

Maurice rocked up and down on his toes and dug his hands into his pockets. "Not exactly. Your show chickens come from special stock, like show calves and sheep, and they need to be raised from baby chicks."

"Huh. Well, we've got no baby chicks, so . . ."

Maurice beamed a smile. "I happen to know a lady who raises 'em. I talked to her this morning and she's got five left. Betty."

"Your wife?"

"Yep, and she says they're the best of the whole lot. She'll give 'em up for five bucks apiece. And we deliver."

"Five bucks! Maurice, you can buy a grown chicken at the grocery store for five bucks, and it's already cut up."

Slim entered the conversation. "Yeah, or you can get ten pounds of frozen turkey necks." Loper and Maurice stared at him. "Well? I eat 'em all the time. They're good, and they're easy to fix, too. You just boil 'em in a big pot for twenty minutes."

Loper shook his head and turned back to Maurice. "Don't pay any attention to him. He's a bachelor. Five bucks for a baby chick is too much."

Maurice pursed his lips and went into deep thought. "Okay, two and a half, just for you, just for the sake of this boy, just because I want him to win grand champion at the fair."

Loper smiled. "Sold. And you deliver?"

"You bet. We deliver 'em in a special cardboard box."

"Good."

"To the front door of my house."

Loper's brows shot up. "We have to pick 'em up? Maurice—"

"Loper, you'll have to buy chicken feed anyway. You can do it all in one trip."

"We've got chicken feed."

Maurice shook his head. "Nope. You need a special show ration. You don't feed regular chicken feed to show birds." Loper groaned. A gleam came into Maurice's eyes. "But you're in luck, because I happen to be the local dealer for Cruncho Feeds."

Loper and Slim exchanged glances, and Loper said, "I never heard of Cruncho Feeds."

"That's because you buy the cheap stuff, Loper. I'm sorry to put it that way, but facts are facts." Maurice reached into the front pocket of his overalls and brought out . . . something made of paper. "Here. Would you like to read a brochure on Cruncho Feeds?"

"No."

"Well, they're the best. They're not cheap, but they're the best. And for that fine boy there, I know you'll want the best."

Loper rubbed the back of his neck and scuffed the ground with his boot. "All right, Maurice, we'll take five chicks and one sack of your hot-rod chicken feed. Add it all up, and I'll write you a check."

"One sack goes pretty fast, Loper."

"All right, *two* sacks. Figure it up."

Maurice seemed deep in thought. "Loper, I don't usually give out this information, but . . . for the past three years, the grand champions in all classes have fed"—he whispered this information behind his hand—"crushed Peruvian oyster shell!"

Loper sighed. "Great. What is it?"

"Well, poultry needs gravel—"

"Gravel for the gizzard, I know all that, Maurice, and we've got miles and miles of sand, rock, and gravel here on the ranch."

Maurice shrugged. "Well, I guess it just depends on what a guy wants. If he wants his child to win a blue ribbon at the fair, he uses the very best gravel money can buy. If he don't care, if an ugly yellow ribbon is good enough—"

"We'll take one sack. Figure it up."

Maurice whipped out a pencil and paper and did some figuring, while Slim grinned and Loper scowled. But then Maurice's head came up. "Oh. I guess you've got a special baby chick self-waterer."

"No. What's wrong with a pie pan?"

"Well" —Maurice gave his head a sad shake— "sometimes the chicks fall in and drown. I just happen to carry—"

"How much?"

"Nineteen ninety-five, plus tax. It's a dandy, sure is."

"Figure it up."

Maurice smiled. "Oh, and we've got liquid vitamins. You put it in their water. You'll sure want those vitamins. Everybody's using 'em."

Loper's face had turned red by this time. "What did chickens do for vitamins back when God was raising them? No vitamins! Figure it up and get out of here."

Maurice figured up the bill and handed it to Loper, whose face turned an even deeper shade of red when he saw the total: $87.49.

Maurice grinned. "Just make the check to

Happy Chick Cruncho Feeds." Maurice turned to Slim. "A guy never regrets buying the best."

Slim nodded and was biting back a smile. "Boy, that's true. If it had been me, I would have bought them vitamins—a whole case."

Loper shot him a killer glare but said nothing.

He ripped the check out of his checkbook and thrust it out to Maurice. "Here. I deducted a buck ninety-five for a hardened steel bolt. That's what it cost me at the John Deere place. And the next time you break down, go somewhere else."

Maurice folded the check and slipped it into his front pocket, climbed up into the cab of the grader, pushed his dog out of the seat, and waved good-bye. "Betty'll have the chicks ready for you. See you at the county fair, Alvin!"

He slammed the door, revved up the motor, and drove off to grade the roads. He seemed proud of himself, and appeared to be telling his dog about it.

Loper glared at the grader, and muttered, "Slim, if you make one smart remark about this, you're fired."

Slim shrugged. "I don't know what you're talking about. I think it'll be a great little project for . . . Alvin."

Slim hurried into the machine shed, leaving

Alfred and Loper alone. Alfred was wearing a puzzled expression. "Dad?"

"Yes, son."

"How come everyone's calling me Alvin?"

Loper looked deeply into his eyes. "They're not very smart. Let's go tell your mother what we've done."

And they walked down to the house, leaving me alone to pulverize my breakfast.

Something Strange in Sally May's Car

There were parts of that conversation I didn't understand, but one part came through loud and clear. Did you happen to notice that Loper bought the best, most expensive hotshot feed for Alfred's chickens—mere birds that nobody had even laid eyes on? Yet when it came to buying food and nourishment for the elite forces of the Security Division . . .

Oh well. As I've said before, in some ways this is a lousy job.

Around four o'clock that afternoon, Little Alfred skipped out the back door of the house, followed a moment later by Sally May. She was carrying Baby Molly and wearing a long face.

Sally May was wearing a long face, that is. Baby Molly wore a short face because she was a baby and babies have small heads and therefore . . . skip it.

On the porch, Sally May looked down at her son and said, "I don't know about this. You and your daddy . . ." That's all she said.

They climbed into the car and drove away. Two hours later, they returned, pulled up into the driveway behind the house, and got out. Sally May was the first to step out of the car. She looked . . . frazzled, shall we say. She wore a dark expression and her hair seemed a bit . . . uh . . . stringy, windblown, disshoveled.

Once outside the car, she muttered, "Why did the air conditioner choose *today* to quit? Idiot." She slammed the door.

Well! That was all I needed to know. Sally May was in a bad mood.

Suddenly I moved my business away from the yard gate and took cover in some tall weeds.

Why would I do such a thing? Well, it's hard to explain. No, it's easy to explain. Sally May and I have had our share of . . . how can I say this? We've had our share of dark times, let us say, and I've learned to pay close attention to her moods. When she's angry, annoyed, unhappy, disgruntled, or irritated, I've found that it's often best if I just . . . well, vanish. Disappear. Hide.

You'd think that the presence of a loyal, friendly, loving dog would improve her mood, but for some reason, it doesn't always work that way. To be honest, there have even been times when I've gotten the feeling that . . . well, she just doesn't like me.

Hard to believe, huh? You bet. And maybe I've been wrong about that. I mean, how could Sally May NOT respond to a dog who is . . . well, loyal, obedient, loving, caring, trusting, courteous, kind, extremely intelligent, perceptive, sensitive, and handsome?

It hardly seemed possible, come to think of it, and suddenly I felt this . . . this *call* in the far corners of my mind, a tiny voice that told me that Sally May was having a bad day and needed a caring, loving dog to share her distress.

Pretty amazing, huh? You bet. I mean, some dogs are sensitive to the needs of their people and some aren't. Those who aren't—your ordinary run of mutts—spend their whole lives stumbling around, grinning, and saying, "Duhhhh." Well, I've never been that kind of dog, and if Sally May needed me for Special Caring Duty, by George, I would answer the call.

I left my hiding place in the weeds and trotted down to the gate. There, I sat down and waited to minister to her needs. I swept my tail across the ground and went into a program we call "Here I Am."

She went around to the other side of the car and opened the door for Little Alfred. "No, we will not keep them in the house."

"But, Mom, they're just wittle bitty, and Dad said—"

"Honey, your father is a wonderful man, but I happen to know that when it's time to clean up a mess, he'll be somewhere else—far, far away." She opened the back door of the car and kept talking. "We'll keep them outside in the yard, where animals belong."

"But, Mom, what if . . ."

I had been listening to this conversation, trying to figure out what they were talking about. None of it made much sense. But then, suddenly, it dawned on me that Sally May had opened the back door of the car . . . and *had left it open*, almost as though . . . gee, was it possible that she had opened it for . . . well, for ME? She wanted me to make a penetration of the car and check something out?

I studied her face and searched for clues that would tell me what I should do next. She went right on talking to Alfred, and seemed hardly even aware of my . . .

Cheep. Cheep. Cheep.

HUH?

Did you hear that? Maybe not, because you weren't there, but I heard it, and let me tell you, fellers, it got my full attention. I switched off the Here I Am Program and went to Full Liftup on all ears. I had two of them.

The point is that my ears shot up. I made tiny adjustments on the Tuning Knob, moved both ears into alignment, and brought the mysterious sound into focus.

Cheep. Cheep. Cheep.

There it was again! Hey, we had some kind of unidentified Something in the back of Sally May's car, and it was alive and making strange sounds! Mice, perhaps? Well, you know where I stand on the issue of Vehicle Security. I'm in charge of all that stuff, securing all the ranch vehicles, and I'm especially concerned about any vehicle used to transport women and children.

Did we allow mice to run loose in Sally May's vehicle? Heck no.

Once again, I turned to Sally May, looking for a sign. She was still talking to Alfred, about a cage or something, and . . . maybe she didn't know she had nasty mice lurking inside her car. Okay, I had no choice but to follow this up on my own. There were . . . uh . . . risks involved. I mean, dogs weren't exactly welcome to enter Sally May's car, but it appeared that the situation demanded a bold plan of action.

Stealthily and stalkingly, I crept toward the open door and peered inside. My goodness, what was going on there? The backseat was loaded down with . . . what was all that stuff? Sacks of feed? Why would . . .

Wait, hold everything, stop right here. Chicken feed! Remember? Maybe you'd forgotten all about the chickens. Not me. Okay, yes, I'd forgotten all about it, to be honest, but that conversation between Loper and Maurice had occurred hours ago.

Don't you get it? Sally May and Little Alfred had driven to the house of Betty and Maurice, and they'd bought some special Cruncho chicken feed. Is it coming back to you now? But the real zinger was that if they'd bought chicken feed, it meant they'd also bought . . .

Cheep. Cheep. Cheep.

. . . it meant they'd brought home . . . slurp, slurp . . . something else.

Uh. Mice. You know how mice love . . . chicken feed.

A cunning squint formed upon my eyes, shall we say, and my gaze drifted over to Sally May. She wasn't watching. Hmmm. I turned back to the interior of the car and, uh, hopped my front feet up on the seat.

Hmmmmm!

There, my eyes fell upon a box, a cute little cardboard box . . . with holes in the sides. And coming from inside the cute little box were . . . uh . . . cute little chirping sounds. Gee whiz, I wondered what could be causing those, uh, sounds. I mean, I had encountered many cardboard boxes in the course of my career, but never one that . . . well, cheeped and chirped.

I cast one more glance toward the, uh, people . . . Sally May and Alfred, shall we say, and they were still deeply involved in their conversation about cages and so forth, and obviously had no time to be bothered with . . .

I inched my way deeper into the car, this time

daring to bring my hind legs off the ground and onto the floorboard. I pointed my nose toward the box. Slurp, slurp. The waterworks of my mouth were suddenly . . . I had to activate Tongulary Pumps to clear out all the water from . . .

I steered my nose to the box and positioned it right under the lid. We had contact! I punched in the commands for Silent Hydraulic Nose Lift, and slowly, very slowly the lid of the box began to . . .

"Hank!"

HUH?

"Get out of my car! Scat! Hike!"

Well, sure. Okay, fine. I had just . . . hey, they'd been busy with other matters, and I'd heard this odd sound coming from . . .

If she didn't want me doing security sweeps of her car, all she had to do was . . . don't forget, *she'd left the door open.* Had I opened the door, broken a window, forced myself into her car? Heck no. I had merely . . . what's a dog supposed to think when they . . .

Okay, fine. I could take a hint. It was clear by this time that Sally May didn't want me inside her car. It made no sense to me, but it was her car, so I did what any normal, healthy American dog would have done.

I scrambled myself underneath the car, and there I proceeded to beam her Sulks and Pouts and Looks of Shattered Dignity.

By George, the next time I heard roars and growls and dangerous noises coming from the backseat of her car, would I rush to check it out, and possibly save her from being attacked and bitten by a bunch of crazed mice? Ha! Not me, never again.

Okay, maybe they weren't exactly "roars and growls and dangerous noises," but they were certainly odd and unusual sounds. But never mind all that. The damage had been done to my pride, and I doubted that I would ever recover from this vote of no confidence.

And for the next several minutes, I gave Sally May a withering display of Pouts and Sulks. I'm not sure I'd ever done a better job. Would you believe that my Pouts and Sulks were so strong, so caustic, that one of the bushes inside the yard dried up, shed its leaves, and died? No kidding. I just roasted that bush.

But you know what? Sally May didn't even notice! She lifted Molly out of the car and went into the house. And suddenly I was alone with my thoughts and my broken reputation, alone and abandoned beneath Sally May's . . .

"Hankie, come here."

A voice? A friendly voice? I squinted my eyes and saw . . . Little Alfred. My pal, my dearest friend. He was inside the yard, sitting on the sidewalk and holding the . . . slurp, slurp . . . holding a cardboard box in his lap, shall we say.

I wiggled my way out from under the car and went to the gate. Duty was calling.

Temptation!

The gate was open, but I didn't dare enter the yard.

Do you understand why? Because Sally May had laws against dogs in her yard, that's why. Now, the cat could come and go as he pleased, loaf all day in the iris patch, mooch scraps, rub on every human leg that passed, and that was all right. But let a dog set foot inside the gate...

She has some weird ideas about dogs, that's all I can figure. She seems to think that if we ever get inside the yard, we'll...I don't know, go nuts or something. Dig holes. Sit on her flowers. Trademark all the shrubberies. Leave big ugly tracks in her flower beds. Beat up her Precious Kitty.

Okay, maybe there was a tiny shred of truth behind her Yard Laws, but only a tiny shred. For the most part, her Yard Laws were insulting to dogs and totally unfair, but I can't let myself get worked up over that.

The point is that I didn't set foot inside the yard. Even though the gate hung open and Little Alfred had summoned me for an important meeting, I stopped on the Dog Side of the gate. I went to Broad Swings on the tail section and waited for further orders.

Alfred saw me there. "Come on in."

I, uh, no thanks. I'd love to, but you know your ma. Better not.

He picked up his box and came over to where I was standing. My ears shot up, and I found myself . . . well, looking closely at the box and . . . sniff, sniff . . . wondering what it might contain.

He gave me a grin. "Want to see what's inside my box?"

Before I knew it, my tongue shot out and sliced across my lips, so to speak, and I beamed him a facial expression that said, "Oh well . . . yeah, sure, why not? Let's see what's inside the . . . uh . . . box."

He lifted the lid and I saw . . .

My ears jumped. My eyes widened. My front paws moved up and down. My tail went into a confused circular pattern of wagging that tried to express . . . that tried NOT to express . . . as I say, it was a confused pattern. And once again, my tongue was working overtime to sweep up all the, uh, water and digestive juices that were suddenly pouring into my mouth.

Chicks. Baby chickens. Five of them. Sitting in the box and staring up at me.

I gave the boy a puzzled look. I mean, didn't he understand that dogs . . . how can I say this so that it doesn't sound too harsh? Didn't he understand that we dogs live under the constant shadow of . . . temptation?

I mean, when a guy rises through the ranks and achieves the position of Head of Ranch Security, he's supposed to be above and beyond the temptations that honk your ordinary run of mutts. *Haunt*, I should say, temptations that haunt the so forth. But the truth of the matter is . . .

Let's try a different approach. We have chickens on the ranch, right? They're adult birds—hens who lay eggs. Sally May shuts them up at night, but during the day they have free run of the place. In other words, I see chickens every day. You'd think that after a while a dog would lose his . . .

This is very hard and you'll have to bear with me. See, I sure wouldn't want the kids to get the wrong idea. I know they kind of admire me, look up to me, and, you know, think of me as a hero, and they'd probably be disappointed if they knew . . . that is, if they *thought* . . .

We're tiptoeing all around this business, aren't we? Okay, it's time take off the gloves, drop all the namby-pamby stuff, and go straight to the bottom line.

Hold on to something steady. This might come as a shock. Here, listen to this.

Temptation

There are times when a dog doesn't know
    how to act.
He gets thoughts in his mind that cause his
    bod to react.
Under certain conditions they could have an
    impact.
It's temptation.
Temptation.

A guard dog's a good dog, down to his boots.
But bad thoughts are a major cause of disputes.
Poison ivy has its poison way down in the roots.

It's temptation.
Temptation.

There's something 'bout a chicken that can
    start a stampede.
In the mind of a dog, it's like planting a seed.
And it grows into something like a noxious
    weed.
It's temptation.
Temptation.

Temptation is a feeling that a dog must contain.
It takes constant supervision with a vigilant
    brain.
When it's out of control, it drives a feller insane.
Temptation. (Slurp, slurp, slurp.)
Temptation. (Slurp, slurp, slurp.)

There! Now it's out in the open. The truth is . . .
the awful truth is that . . . I HAVE A TERRIBLE
WEAKNESS FOR CHICKEN!!!

I said it, and now you're shocked and disappointed. But there's more to this confession. It
gets worse before it gets awful.

Can I go on with this? I've got to try.

Okay, here's the deal. In my daily comings and
goings around the ranch, I see chickens every day,

doing the things you would expect a brainless bird to do. They peck gravel, chase grasshoppers, and cluck. No big deal there, no surprises. But even though I see chickens every day, there's something really strange about the way . . .

I don't see them as they actually are, but as . . . meals. Food. Dinner.

It's true. When I see a fat hen scratching up gravel in front of the machine shed, I don't see her with feathers and feet. I see her . . . *on a plate*! On a plate with mashed potatoes and gravy, green peas, and a tossed salad! With fragrant waves of chickenness hovering in the air!

It's a terrible thing, this trick my mind plays upon my body, but I just can't seem to change the picture. It goes on and on, day after day . . . chicken dinners walking around in front of me, chicken dinners waiting to be eaten, chicken dinners . . .

Now you know the darkness that follows me around every day, the dreadful specter of temptation that lurks inside my heart and mind.

But Little Alfred didn't understand, and when he lifted the lid on the cardboard box, I found myself staring at . . . five little chicken dinners . . . sitting on five plates . . . with five big helpings of mashed potatoes and gravy.

Slurp, slurp.

I beamed him a look of Greatest Urgency. I had to get the message across to him: "Alfred, son, what we're doing here isn't good. It's very bad. You need to close the lid and take the box inside the house . . . somewhere . . . anywhere . . . but get it out of here!"

He wasn't even looking at me. He missed it all. He was admiring his new . . . uh . . . pets. "See what I've got, Hankie? Five wittle chickies. I'm gonna waise 'em to be gwown chickens, and then I'm gonna win me a wibbon at the county fair."

His eyes came up and focused on me. He seemed to be waiting for a response of some kind. With tail wags and facial expressions, I managed to say, "Oh. Yes. Chickies. That's nice. Very nice."

The boy went on. "We're gonna keep 'em in a cage in the yard, Hankie, and I'm gonna wet you *guard 'em.*"

HUH?

Me? Guard the chickies?

My gaze wandered away. For some reason, I found it hard to . . . well, look him in the eyes, shall we say.

He continued. "And if the coyotes come up in the night, you bark and wun 'em off, okay?"

For a moment of heartbeats, I found myself

alone with my . . . uh . . . thoughts. There were many of them. Unfortunately, I'm not at liberty to . . . uh . . . discuss them. Sorry.

I turned back to the boy and gave him a broad, toothy . . . that is, I gave him a pleasant smile that said, "Sure, that'll work. No problem. It's just part of the . . . heh-heh . . . job, right? You bet. No coyote will ever get a chance to eat those little guys . . . and that's a promise. Heh-heh."

So there it was. I had been assigned to Special Chickie Guarding Duty, and I must admit that I was honored and flattered that my little pal had . . . uh . . . selected me out of all the dogs in the world to handle this special task.

And once I took over the job, he sure didn't need to worry about coyotes gobbling down his little friends. No sir! Not coyotes, nor skunks nor badgers nor coons nor great horned owls. Once the Head of Ranch Security was on the job, he didn't need to worry about . . .

You remember that stuff we discussed, the business about temptation and chicken dinners and so forth? Ha-ha. Nothing to it. Honest. It was just . . . gossip. Nonsense. A momentary leap into the world of fantasy, shall we say.

It was a joke, just a harmless little joke.
Ha-ha.

So don't give it another thought. In fact, I'd appreciate it if you'd just forget we ever mentioned it, because . . . well, because we didn't. You thought we discussed my so-called weakness for chicken dinner, but you were probably misquoted. What I meant to say . . . what I actually *did* say was that Heads of Ranch Security are above temptation, and we have no weakness for . . . uh . . . you know, chickies and so forth.

No kidding.

Everything was fine and under control.

Where were we? Oh yes, I had just been named Guardian of the Chickies, and after the ceremonies, Little Alfred and his mother went to work preparing a house for my . . . that is, for the chickies. They hiked up the hill to the machine shed and found a little chicken coop, and hauled it down to the . . .

I was sitting by the yard gate, minding my own business and watching the preparations and so forth, and all at once I got this creepy feeling that . . . that Sally May was *staring at me.* No, it was worse than that. She seemed to be looking into my mind and soul, almost as though . . .

Have we discussed Sally May and her X-ray Eyes? Maybe not. Well, she's got these eyes that don't just glide over the surface of things. They drill and bore and penetrate into the dipper deefs ... the deeper depths, shall we say, and they always seem to be looking for ...

Naughty thoughts.

It has something to do with Motherhood. Mothers seem to be suspicious of all dogs and little boys, don't you see, and they have these X-ray Eyes that are equipped to ignore the surface details and to probe the dipper deefs. I mean, a careless smile that would fool Slim or Loper doesn't have a chance against that woman. She's relentless. Her eyes have the nose of a bloodhound.

That sounds odd, doesn't it, but it just goes to prove that she . . . well, she makes me nervous. And even though I had nothing to hide, even though I hadn't hosted a naughty thought in . . . well, days or weeks or even months, I couldn't shake the feeling that she was . . . *reading my mind.*

And that gave me a creepy feeling, so I, uh, found it convenient ... that is, it suddenly occurred to me that I needed to check on Drover. Remember Drover? I had sent him to his room to sit on a sticker and suffer, and by George, I needed to, uh, check on him. No kidding.

So I left my spot beside the yard gate and

hiked myself down to the gas tanks. Thirty yards south of the gate, I finally placed myself beyond the reach of her radar. Whew! Only then was I able to relax.

You might want to make a note of this. Motherly Radar is deadly accurate up to a range of thirty yards, but beyond that . . . heh-heh . . . little boys and dogs are free to think whatever they wish.

Although I must hasten to point out that I had nothing to hide, almost nothing at all. No kidding.

You won't be surprised that I found Drover asleep on his gunnysack bed, and we're talking about conked out—snoring, quivering, twitching, squeaking, and doing all the other bizarre things he does in his sleep.

I stood over him for a moment, marveling at all the noise. Then I eased my nose down to the level of his left ear and shifted into a little routine we call "Alarm Clock." We use it to pry slackers and loafers out of their, heh-heh, slumber.

I yelled, *Wake up and spit, the world's on fire!*

CHAPTER ELEVEN

I Try to Help Drover

I must admit that I get wicked pleasure out of waking up Drover. You should have seen the little mutt. He started scrambling all four legs, but since he was lying on his side, he didn't move an inch. One ear shot up, and his eyes popped open, revealing . . . well, not much. When he's half asleep, Drover's eyes contain a vast nothingness.

And now that you mention it, they contain the same vast nothingness when he's awake.

"Help, murder, Mayday! Fire, fire! Spit on the fire and put out the galloping pork chops!"

Heh-heh. This was fun.

After a moment or two of Stationary Stampede, he finally made it to his feet. He staggered around in circles, then recognized me. "Oh, hi. How's the fire?"

"Fine, thanks. How about yourself?"

"Oh . . . I'm not sure. I think I just woke up."

"Exactly my point, Drover. If you just woke up, it means that you were asleep."

"Yeah, 'cause the awaker you are, the asleeper you used to be."

"Say that again?"

"I said . . . the asleeper you are, the awaker . . . I'm not sure what I said."

"It doesn't matter. The point is"—I began pacing, as I often do when I'm conducting a heavy interrogation—"if you've been down here sleeping, you weren't suffering for your crimes. I sent you down here to stick on a stuffer and sucker."

He rolled his eyes around. "You mean, suck on a sticker and suffer?"

"Yes, exactly. That's what I just said. Don't make me repeat myself."

"What?"

"I said, stop repeating myself. Now, did you suck on the sticker or sit on it? We need to get to the bottom of this."

"Well, let me think here." He twisted his

mouth into a thoughtful pose. "I sat my bottom on the sucker, and my hiney still hurts. Does that sound right?"

"Good, good!"

"What's good? It hurt like crazy."

"Yes, but that's the whole point of spitting on a sticker, Dricker. You suffered. Under certain conditions, suffering is good for us."

"Yeah, but my name's Drover."

I stopped pacing. "What?"

"You called me 'Dricker.'"

"I did not call you Dricker. Why would I have called you Dricker? Dricker isn't even a word."

"Yeah it is. If it wasn't a word, you couldn't have said it."

"I didn't say it. I said 'suffer.'"

"No, you said 'sticker,' and then you called me Dricker."

I heaved a sigh and looked up at the sky. "I came down here for a reason. I came to watch you suffer, Druffer, and now you've got me so confused, I don't know whether it's raining or Tuesday."

"Well, I think it's Thursday, but last week was March and my name's still Drover."

I marched over to him and stickered my nose in his fose. "Why do you keep saying that? I know your name! Do you need proof? Okay, here. Drover, Drover, Drover, Drover!"

"What, what, what, what?"

"I know your name."

"Then how come you keep calling me Dricker and Druffer?" He lowered his head and began to snucker...sniffle, that is. "And I wish you wouldn't yell at me. You know I can't stand to be yelled at in the morning."

"I'm not yelling!" I yelled. "And besides, it's not morning. It's . . ." Suddenly I realized that nothing we were saying made any sense. I heaved a sigh and marched a few steps away, allowing the toxic vapors to clear from wreckage of my mind. "Drover, listen carefully."

"Thanks for calling me Drover."

"Shut up. Did you fulfill your quota of suffering or not? I must know."

"What was the quota?"

"One hour of sticker pain."

He smiled through his tears. "Yep, I sure did. Are you proud of me?"

"I'll be prouder, Drouder, if you've learned a lesson about the dangers of temptation. Temptation stalks all dogs, and we must be strong."

He burst into tears.

"Ah! I've exposed something here. Do you want to tell me about it?"

"Yes!" he cried through his tears. "You called me . . . Drouder!"

"You said I called you Dricker. Get your stories straight. Dricker or Drouder, Drover, you can't have it both ways."

"Help!" Before my very eyes, the runt crawled beneath his gunnysack, leaving nothing but his hiney exposed and sticking straight up in the air. "I'm so confused!"

"Come out of there!"

"No, I can't stand this anymore! I don't even know my own name!"

"Ah, there it is! You don't know your own name, but you're trying to transfer the blame onto me. You're a sick dog, Drogger, and I'm not sure we can save you."

"Help!"

"This is much worse than I thought." My mind was racing. "Okay, try this. Take two aspens and go back to bed."

One corner of the gunnysack lifted, and I saw an eye peering out at me. "We don't have any aspens. What about cottonwoods?"

"They're trees."

"Oh, good. Thanks, Hank. I'm feeling better already."

I stood over him for a moment, looking down at this weird little guy we knew as Drover. Clearly, he had some pretty serious problems, but maybe our session had pulled him through the worst of it. I hoped so. In many ways, he was a nice little lunatic, yet beneath the many layers of garbage in his mind, there lurked a wasteland.

I heaved a sigh, beamed him one last look of fatherly concern, and made my way up the hill. The evening sun was drifting down on the horizon, like a mother hen settling down on her nest.

Slurp.

Which, uh, reminded me that darkness was coming, and that I had a very important job waiting for me. Yes, it would be a tough assignment, perhaps the toughest of my whole career. Tender chickies cheeping in the darkness of night would bring all manner of villains into headquarters, all of them lusting for a chicken dinner.

Would I be able to fight them off and save the little chickies?

In this moment of quiet before the battle began, I turned to the vast computer screen of my mind and called up the Villains Program. I browsed my way through the names and faces of all the villains in our files: Rip, Snort, Scraunch the Terrible, Sinister the Bobcat, Buster and Muggs, Wallace and Junior, Eddy the Rac.

And then I studied the mug shots of other villains whose names we didn't know: various skunks, badgers, raccoons, bobcats, chicken hawks, and owls, any one of whom might be the one to attack my, uh, chickies.

Which would it be? Who would be the villain I would have to face in the grim darkness of night?

I saw his face in my mind.

I even knew his name.

Yes, I knew who the villain would be. I knew him very well. We had, uh, spent a lot of time together, shall we say, but I'm afraid I can't reveal his identity.

Security reasons, don't you see.

CHAPTER TWELVE

The Killer Strikes!

Darkness fell like a curtain of darkness around the edges of the ... something. Darkness fell, shall we say, as it always does at a certain time of day, usually in the late afternoon or evening. It happens every day.

In other words, the coming of darkness was no big surprise because it happens all the time, but on this particular occasion, there was a certain ... a certain tension in the air. I could feel it in my bones. Not in the various steak and beef bones I had buried around the ranch, but in the bones of my own ...

There was tension in the air, and I could feel it in my bones. It was a strange sensation. I had a feeling, an odd, eerie, unsplickable feeling that ...

something was about to happen. It was a feeling of dread, a sense of four boating.

Foreboding, let us say. Somewhere out there in the darkness, some slouching, brooding creature was watching ... listening ... plotting ...

Pretty spooky, huh? You bet it was. But the good part in all this scary stuff was that ... well, I would be right there at the yard gate to, uh, guard and protect the little slurp-slurps ... the little chickies, shall we say. And hey, when Hank is there to guard the chickens, what could possibly ... uh ... happen?

At ten o'clock, Little Alfred came out of the house for the last time. He'd been cheeking the chuckies every fifteen minutes, don't you see, but now it was his bedtime. Checking the chickies, let us say, making sure they were safe and sound, healthy and yummy ... healthy and *warm*, that is.

And at ten o'clock, everything seemed fine. Dressed in his polka-dot pajamas, Alfred came over to my sentry post near the yard gate. He seemed worried, concerned. He squinted out into the spooky deepness of the dark, then let out a sigh.

"Welp, I've got to go to bed, Hankie. Weckon my chickies will be okay?"

Oh sure. No problem. Let the rascals come! By

George, if the ruffians wanted to test the elite troops of the Security Division, let 'em try it!

He opened the gate and stepped over to me. He put his arms around my . . . gulk . . . neck and gave me a big hug. "Hankie, pwomise you'll take care of my chickies?"

I looked him straight in the eyes, raised my right paw in the air, and swore a sodden oath: "Alfred, of all the dogs in this world, I'm one of them. If anything should happen to your chickies, I'll be the first to know about it. You have my word on that."

This seemed to put his mind at ease. He smiled, closed the gate, and said, "Well, nightie night. See you in the morning."

I licked my . . . that is, I raised my paw in a gesture of farewell.

I watched him go into the house. The door closed behind him. Moments later, the lights began going off, one by one. The house grew dark and silent. At lone, I was alast with my . . . at last I was alone with my thoughts, let us say, and several of those thoughts were . . . uh . . . pretty interesting.

A quiver of anticipation made its way down my backbone and out to the end of my tail. I cast a slow glance to my left and then to my right, just to be sure . . . I was indeed alone. Nobody would ever see . . . nobody would ever know . . .

It was then that my eyes fell upon the, uh, cage. Lick, slurp. It sat upon the ground and against the side of the house, just to south of the porch. Inside the cage were five tender, sleeping . . . oh, by the way, have we ever done our "Guarding the Chickies" song? Heck of a song. Here's how it goes.

Guarding the Chickies

Part One: Chickies
Tender chickies safe and warm
There is naught can do us harm.

Windows bolted, doors are locked,
We're secure inside our box.

Sleeping chickies, safe within,
Guarded by a watchful friend.

Part Two: Hank
Tender little chicken strips, helpless in
    a box.
Villains lurking in the darkness,

testing all the locks.
Yummy, juicy pullybones, drumsticks,
and thighs.
Predators are watching them with
hunger in their eyes.

Bad things happen all the time, many
things go wrong.
Someone leaves the door unlocked, and
poof! The chicks are gone.

Pretty inspiring song, huh? You bet.

My ears shot up, and before I realized it, my tail was tapping out an urgent message on the ground, telling me that it was time to . . . well, check things out, as you might say.

Heh-heh.

I cut my eyes from side to side and raised my enormous body to its full height. I felt myself moving toward the fence: step, step, step. Upon reaching the fence, I went into the Deep Crouch Formation, took careful note of the height of the fence, and sent all the targeting information straight to Data Control's massive mainframe computer.

Tense and quivering with excitement, I waited for Clearance. At last it came: *"Launch the weapon!*" Without a hessant's momentation . . . a moment's hesitation, that is, I launched myself into the air, cleared the fence as gracefully as a deer, and made a soft landing on the other side.

I had just entered Her Yard, an action that . . . well, caused me to feel a certain amount of anxiety and . . . okay, might as well admit it . . . guilt. Even though I had entered Sally May's precious yard to provide security for the tender, juicy little chickies . . . for Little Alfred's county fair chickens, let us say, I couldn't help feeling a few prickles of . . . **guilt**.

You know how it is between me and Sally May. Just the thought of her makes me feel . . . but on the other hand, I was there on an errand of mercy, right? If Sally May had been consulted about this, I'm sure she would have wanted me to stay close to the chicken dinners . . . to the chickies . . . the county fair chickens. Right? Sure she would have.

With narrowed eyes, I conducted one last Visual Sweep of the yard and surrounding territory. All clear. I took a gulp of fresh air and hurried across lawny grass, until I found myself standing right beside the serving line . . . the cage, that is, the cage that held the very chickens I had been, uh, hired to guard.

Sniff, sniff.

Slurp, lick, slorp.

Yes, they were inside the cage, peeping slee-fully . . . sleeping peacefully. That was good. Growing drumsticks . . . that is, growing *chickens* needed their, uh, sleep.

I eased my nose toward the top of the cage and began studying the little door. There was this little door on top, don't you see, and it was equipped with a kind of latching device that . . . heh-heh . . . would be no problem at all. I mean, any dog with a strong nose would have no problem easing the latch . . .

I heard a sound off to my left, near the yard gate. I whirled around and listened. A voice came floating through the still night air: "Hank? What are you doing in the yard?"

The air hissed out of my body. It was Drover. I crept over to the fence. "You're supposed to be in your room, suffering."

"Yeah, but I got bored and I just wondered . . . you're not thinking of doing what I think you're thinking of doing . . . are you?"

I cut my eyes from side to side. "I guess that depends on what you're thinking, Drover, but the short answer is no. I'm on duty, guarding the dinners . . . the chickens . . . Alfred's chickens."

"Oh, good. There for a minute, I was afraid . . . you wouldn't eat his chickens, would you?"

"Drover, I'm shocked and aslurpished . . . astonished that you'd even ask such a question."

"Yeah, but what's the answer?"

"The answer is, go back to bed and stop worrying. I gave you my lecture on temptation, didn't I?"

"Yeah, but—"

"Well, nothing more needs to be said. We must be aware of temptation at all times and guard ourselves against . . . I've got everything under control, Drover."

"Well," he yawned, "okay. I guess I'll shuffle on to bed."

"Great. Sweet dreams."

By the time his footsteps had vanished in the darkness, my whole body was quivering with anticipation. I rushed back to the cage and . . .

HUH?

. . . found myself staring in the face of . . . A CAT! It was Pete! He was sitting on top of the cage and had just opened the door . . . and was about to reach his paw inside!

He grinned and fluttered his eyes. "Mmmm. Hello, Hankie. I was watching you. I saw everything."

For a moment I was too shocked to squeak.

Speak. "You saw nothing, Kitty, because there was nothing to see. I'm guarding these dinners ... chickens ... I'm guarding Little Alfred's chickies, you little sneak, and maybe you'd like to explain why your paw is inside the cage."

He stared at me with hooded eyes. "You know what I'm doing, Hankie. I just beat you to it."

"Lies, Pete, lies. I don't know what you're talking about."

"Sure you do. What would you say about a fifty-fifty split? Half for you and half for me? I mean, I'm almost inside the cage and you're not even close."

"Pete, I'm shocked that you'd even . . . fifty-fifty, huh?" My mind was racing. "Well, I guess we might ... wait a second, hold everything! How can you split five chickens into two equal parts?"

Pete let out a gasp. "Why, I hadn't thought of that, Hankie. You're better at math than I thought."

"Right, and don't you ever forget it either."

"Well" —a cunning look passed over his face— "I guess one of us will get two and the other will get ... three."

"Now you're talking, pal. I'll get the three I deserve, and you'll take two."

His smile faded, and I noticed that the tip of

his tail was twitching back and forth. "No, no, Hankie. That won't work."

"Hey, Pete, I was here first."

"Yes, but I'm the one who's small enough to slip inside the cage. You're too"—he fluttered his eyes—"fat. Too fat, too bad. I tried to make a deal, Hankie."

And with that, he . . . you won't believe this . . . before my very eyes, the little sneak of a chicken-stealing thief eased himself through the opening and slithered inside the cage!

"Pete, you're disgusting! This is an outrage! I can't believe you'd . . ."

It was then that I realized . . . suddenly a bold and clever plan began to glow in the dark corners of my mind. Suddenly I realized that . . . well, eating Little Alfred's chickies would be a terrible thing to do, right? And I'd been given the job of protecting them from coyotes and skunks and . . .

Okay, remember that moment earlier in the day when I'd had this . . . this vision, this powerful feeling that some heartless villain would try to eat our Precious Chickies? At the time, I'd thought it might be Rip and Snort or Scraunch, Sinister the Bobcat, or one of the usual suspects on the ranch, but it had never occurred to me . . .

Somehow I had omitted the name of the most

likely suspect of all, the most cunning, the most greedy and selfish, the most heartless villain of all.

Pete the Barncat.

Do you get it now? Pete had been planning this deal all along, and somehow I had . . . well, picked up the mental thought patterns of his so forth. Yes, I had known, in my deepest heart of hearts, that our chickies, our dear Precious Chickies, would be attacked by this greedy little fiend!

And suddenly I realized that . . . hey, Pete was inside the chicken coop! I sprang forward, shot out my right front paw, and slammed the door shut.

I looked into Pete's astonished eyes. He wasn't grinning anymore. "Now, Hankie, let's don't do anything we might regret. Maybe we could—"

"Forget it, Pete. You ought to know that I never do business with creeps like you. I'm afraid your chickens have come home to roost."

And with that, I went straight into an emergency barking program we call "Alert and Alarm." Suddenly the thieving, sneaking cat was flying around inside the cage, bouncing off the walls and scattering baby chicks in all directions.

I barked with all my heart and soul. "Alert, alert! Alarm, alarm! May I have your attention, please! We have just trapped a killer cat in the chicken coop! Send all troops and angry ranch wives to the backyard at once!"

The lights came on inside the house. I heard the murmur of voices and the sounds of feet upon the floor. The yard light came on, the back door flew open, and out came . . . everybody. Alfred, Loper, and Sally May.

Fellers, it was one of the finest moments of my career. There, in the glare of the yard light, they saw the Head of Ranch Security, pointing like a bird dog at the chicken coop, inside of which lurked the villainous, bloodthirsty cat who had attempted this awful crime.

Tee-hee.

You should have seen Kitty Kitty. By this time, he was huddled in a corner of the cage, glaring daggers at me with his weird cattish eyes. His ears were pinned down on his head and . . . you'll love this part . . . he had a chickie roosting on his head!

Sally May almost fainted in shock when she saw her spoiled, pampered kitty curled up in the cage. "Pete! How could you . . ."

There was a throbbing moment of silence. Then, Little Alfred said, "Hankie saved my chickens! Pete was twying to eat 'em!"

Hard lines formed on Sally May's brow. She beamed me a suspicious look (what had I done?), then marched over to the cage, snapped open the door, and dragged Mister Chicken Stealer out by the scruff of his neck.

She held him up for all the world to see (I loved it) and said, "Pete, you naughty, naughty cat! The very idea! Shame on you, shame, shame, shame!"

Hee-hee, ho-ho, ha-ha.

It was wonderful, delicious! I loved every second of it! Pete got the tongue-lashing of his life, got pitched out of the yard, and received the humbling he so richly deserved. And me?

Well, what can I say? I had caught the villain, saved the little chickies, and solved the case, all in the space of fifteen minutes. There in the backyard, in the spotlight, in front of everyone, I received the Bronze Star and the Ranchonal Medal of Honor, and was even named Dog of the Year.

No kidding. And you know what else? *Sally May heaped praise upon me!* Here's what she said, word for word. She said, "I don't know what went on out here but . . . all right, Hank, somehow you've blundered into doing the right thing. Good dog."

Did you hear that? GOOD DOG! From Sally May!

Wow! What a night! Well, it doesn't get any better than that, does it? And when it doesn't get any better, it's time to shut 'er down and call it a day.

Case closed.

P.S. I never would have harmed those precious little chickies. Honest. And all that stuff about chicken dinners? Nothing to it. Just a little joke. Ha-ha. No kidding.

Oh. Alfred's and my chickens grew up and won two ribbons at the county fair. Boy, I was sure proud of those . . . slurp slurp . . . chickies.

The following activities are samples from *The Hank Times*, the official newspaper of Hank's Security Force. Do not write on these pages unless this is your book. Even then, why not just find a scrap of paper?

"Photogenic" Memory Quiz

We all know that Hank has a "photogenic" memory—being aware of your surroundings is an important quality for a Head of Ranch Security. Now you can test your powers of observation.

How good is your memory? Look at the illustration on page 8 and try to remember as many things about it as possible. Then turn back to this page and see how many questions you can answer.

1. Was the frog on a lily pad or on the land?

2. How many wires were on the fence? 2, 3, or 4?

3. Were Hank's ears pointing up or down?

4. The frog was catching one fly. How many more flies were there?

5. Was Drover doing the dog paddle or the backstroke?

6. How many of Hank's eyes could you see? 1, 2, or 3?

The Missing Sausage Mystery

I t's me again, Hank the Cowdog. Slim had just tossed me a Little Piggie Sausage, and I was about to scoop it up in my enormous jaws when suddenly I heard something. I turned around but didn't see anything. I turned back to find that my sausage was gone! I need your help in finding the culprit.

As Head of Ranch Security, I'm opening a full-scale investigation into this mystery. Can you help me solve it with these clues?

As you go through the clues, keep in mind that there are true clues and false clues. **Only clues that can be verified by what you can see are true clues.** If there is a clue that requires you to hear, touch, smell, or taste, it is a false clue.

Read each clue carefully. Put the clue number beside a character's name when a clue eliminates that character as a suspect. Some clues may eliminate more than one character, but don't let a false clue eliminate a character or you may let the real culprit go free. Help Hank find out who swiped his sausage.

1. The suspect does not have ears pointing down.
2. The suspect said he wanted his mommy.
3. The suspect was not wearing a cowboy hat.
4. The suspect smelled like rotten meat.
5. The suspect was howling like a dog.
6. The suspect was looking to his right.

The culprit is _____

Slim_____   Alfred_____   Drover_____

Pete_____   The Pasha of Shizzam_____

Have you read all of Hank's adventures?